To Helen,
Joel -

CW00862715

# THE EARTH CHRONICLES

# Hannah
## and the
# Hollow
# Tree

Enjoy with a brew...

Love -

## J. A. BROWNE

Jane .
xo .

For Mum and for Dad

*"…our contract with Earth is fundamental, for we are part of it and cannot survive without a healthy planet as our home."*

James Lovelock,
*Gaia: A New Look at Life on Earth*

First published in Great Britain in 2018 by Peahen Publishing Ltd
www.peahenpublishing.com

Copyright © 2018 J. A. Browne
Illustrated by Darran Holmes

ISBN: 978-1-9999016-5-3

All rights reserved. No part of this book may be reproduced, stored
in a retrieval system, or transmitted in any form or by any means
electronic, mechanical, photocopying, recording or otherwise,
without the prior permission of the publisher and copyright owner.

A CIP catalogue record for this is available from the British Library

Peahen
Publishing
Bringing your stories to life

THE EARTH CHRONICLES

# Hannah
### and the
# Hollow
# Tree

J. A. BROWNE

# *Prologue*
# Flooded Dreams

Water rises, covering each step within seconds.

"What are we going to do?" I scream.

"Back up! Back up!" Mum orders.

In pyjamas and boots, hoodies and hats we race up to the top floor. The house groans and creaks. Windows crack then shatter against the weight of the water. In the distance, the siren sounds. Floods are something you get used to in York … but this is something else.

Mum jumps up onto her bed and pulls the blind, filling the room with the hazy glow of moonlight. Yanking on the window's bar, Mum opens it wide into a tilt letting the thick rain lash us.

"We're going out there? You've gotta be kiddin'?" I shout, peeling strands of hair from my face. My old Year 6 Leavers' hoodie turns from light to dark grey.

"Hannah, get up here. Now!"

*The water's rising way too fast. This can't be real.*

Seeping under Mum's bedroom door, the floodwater saturates the carpet. I have no choice. Stepping up, I place my hands on the cold plastic of the window ledge. Mum takes my leg and I push off from her as she balances on the bed. Straining, I pull myself up.

"Hurry, Hannah!"

The panic in her voice sends a lightning rod through me. Once up, I straddle the ledge, then lean down to Mum. Gripping my hand, she bounces on the bed jumping as high as possible. I claw at her clothes as she heaves herself up onto the window's ledge, safe from the rising waters. Lying flat on her stomach, she reaches to grab the metal bar pulling herself up and out. Wind whips her rain mac over her head. I yank it back as we straddle the velux window like jockeys. Glancing back down as we cling to each other, we watch floodwater lapping against her bed. In no time at all it's lifted from the floor making a raft of it.

"Mum, shouldn't we go back down and get on the bed?"

"No. Too dangerous."

"More dangerous than *this*?"

Looking out, neighbours line their own rooftops as the floodwater continues to rise swallowing anything below the guttering. *How is this happening?* Old Mr Joseph at No. 11 wouldn't have stood a chance. *At least we've got the moonlight.*

"Mum, what do we do? The water's still rising!"

"I know, sweetheart." Mum shakes her head, her blonde hair matted to her face.

"Listen!" A whirring sound drones in the distance. "It might be the coastguard! Or the air ambulance!"

From my hoodie, I pull out my phone, swipe up and press the torch icon.

"Good thinking!" Mum says. She pads her mac down, searching for her own. "Damn!" she adds. Looking down from our skylight position, we watch her phone bob along the water's surface until it sinks without a trace.

"It'll be okay. Look!" I say.

Up the street dozens of people are holding their phones up, torch apps blaring, hopeful.

"I think the water's slowing," Mum says watching her new divan float from one side of her room to the other.

"What about jumping to the tree? It's a massive oak and it's not that far."

Mum's calculation face kicks in, but we don't have time for that.

"Mum, come on!"

She takes my phone and puts it in the inside pocket, zipping it shut. It's the only lifeline we have. Carefully, we push ourselves up and out onto the roof, shuffling our boots against the slippery slate tiles. Clothes, soaked, stick to our limbs. The smell of stagnant water and sewage begins to rise as the rain stings our cheeks and cold hands. Flattening ourselves closer to the roof, I shuffle behind Mum as she checks for loose roof tiles. *It only takes one.* Eventually, we reach the far edge of the house, having travelled barely more than a few metres to the nearest point to the oak. I curl up into a crouched position at the very edge of the rooftop. Mum prays out loud that the guttering doesn't snap.

"I think I should go first, Hannah. Then you can jump to me and I'll catch you."

"No! Don't leave me. Please, don't leave me, Mum!"

I grab her hand. She sighs, looking lost. "Then you'll have to jump first. We only have two options, Hannah and we're running out of time."

*No! I can't.*

The whirring blades of a helicopter grow closer. As I cling to Mum, she waves her arms. Its searchlight scans the rooftops for signs of life, stopping across the street where, incredibly, Eva from No.8 clings to the rooftop; her cat's head popping out from her knitting bag. *She's 79! If Eva can do this, I can.*

Fighting against the backdraft from the air ambulance, we flatten ourselves to the roof, as its searchlight swings across to us. "The coastguard are on their way," a voice blares out from a megaphone.

I watch Eva and her cat, Mr Nibbles, being hoisted to safety. Thank God. The helicopter angles back, pulling away from dozens more people shouting and pleading for help, but the whirring blades fade.

Suddenly, the house shakes and groans and begins to sway.

*Time's up.*

"Hannah, jump!"

But I can't. Fear has paralysed my legs. I look across to the oak tree. Help me, please!

The oak shakes its huge canopy, shedding its autumn colours as if it's heard me. Branches bend their elbows and unfold from their joints, opening wide. The oak leans forward …

*Flash.*

A streak of emerald and gold shoots through the tree's veins, illuminating it. Its glow is so warm. I realise the rain has stopped. Bending its trunk and lowering its crown of green, it bows.

*Flash.*

*What was that?*

*Am I dreaming?*

"Hannah, you can do this! Please, jump!" Mum cries.

*Can she see what the tree's doing?*

The oak stretches its branches like fingertips awaiting my touch.

*Heart pounding.*

I jump.

Flinging my arms wide, branches flex and catch me. The oak pulls me in close to the trunk and I grapple to hold on. It clutches my ankle guiding my foot to a branch to balance on. *Incredible!*

"Please save my mum," I whisper pressing fingers against the ridges of its bark.

I look back to see her teetering on the edge of the house. Without warning the oak tree lifts from its foundations – Mum leaps – branches reach out for her …

"Hold on!" I scream.

Mum grabs a clutch of its thin limbs, but plunges into the water. Branches spring back up from the depths … she's gone … Mum's gone …

## CHAPTER ONE

# 30th October 2021: Hannah
### 3 a.m.

What is it about phone calls in the middle of the night that always makes people nervous? I press my stomach in the hope that it stops curdling like week-old milk. I am covered in cold, clammy sweat, drenched in fact. Like I was drowning or something.

*Is that what my dream was about?*

Sometimes dreams feel so real, don't they?

I shove the weight of the 13.5 tog duvet – Mum insisted I have – down to my shins, before pressing my fingertips into the cool pools of sweat that sits in the well of my collarbone. Upstairs, I can hear Mum's muffled voice.

*I've got to change that foghorn ringtone of hers.*

I wince against the brightness of my mobile as my eyes adjust. *Who soddin' well rings at 3 a.m.? I mean, it's not going to be anyone with good news, is it?*

I close the case and stick it back in the dock, before lying back and pulling the matted hair from the back of my neck up onto my pillow. Sometimes rain is soothing to listen to. But not tonight. It reminds me of the dream, I can't quite remember. Like a lion tamer's whip, the wind and rain lash the windowpanes as if trying to scar the glass.

*Huh!*

Flashes fill my room.

*One-one-thousand. Two-one-thousand. Three …*

The starving thunder rumbles ever closer. *How on earth did I sleep through that?* Normally, I'm such a light sleeper. *Weird. Not like me.* It's closing in. We never used to get many thunderstorms in Yorkshire, but now … and rain, well, that we get by the bucket load. I've never liked thunder since I was little. Mum used to say it was the gods arguing with each other. I never actually asked her which gods she meant though. Her meant-to-comfort story doesn't work now, of course. I'm not a little kid anymore, but still, I curl into a ball and roll onto my side. Between each rumble I listen for Mum's footsteps from above because they'll tell me if it's bad news or no news.

There it is … a slight creak, like an unhinged gate.

I track her footsteps across my ceiling; ancient floorboards in an ancient house. She crosses her room back and forth, dresser drawers being pulled open then slid shut. Eventually, her footsteps descend the narrow attic staircase and my heart sinks like a badly skimmed stone across a pond. Bad news, then. My door edges open and I wait for Mum to speak.

"Hannah?"

I bolt up onto my knees, balancing on the edge of the bed. There's an urgency in her voice causing a sudden flush of goose bumps across my arms. I watch her flick on the lamp; her face a mixture of tiredness and ... shock, maybe?

"What's happened? I heard the phone."

Stomach somersaults begin ...

"Always been a light sleeper, Han." *Apparently not tonight, though.*

"Mum, what's happened?"

But Mum just says, "Get dressed, Han, okay?" as she pulls a jumper, jeans and underwear from my dresser. "Here."

She resumes her default setting, otherwise known as 'ABM' – Automatic Bee Mode. Clothes fly from drawer to bed. My purple roll neck clings to the duvet like a mountaineer, before eventually dropping to the floor. I just stare at her busying herself. If she's thinking about other things, then she isn't thinking about ... *What the hell's happened?*

She balls up a pair of slipper socks and glances back at me. "Sweetheart, seriously. I need you to get dressed. Now. We have to go."

"But why?"

Her blue eyes narrow, then she turns away and is still for moment. Mum unhooks her hair from behind her ears, creating a blonde veil between us, which usually means the urge to cry is rising.

She swallows hard. "We have to go."

"What do you mean, 'We have to go.' Where?"

"Norwich."

*Norwich? But that's …*

"Oh my God, Gran! Is she okay? What's happened?"

Mum doesn't reply. She's in her head, not in my room. I climb off the bed and stand by her side.

"Mum! Is Gran okay?"

She's wearing her 'calculation face', like she's still mathematically weighing up what the caller said. Something then equalises because she replies, "I don't know, love," before pressing the balled up pair of socks into my hand. "Just get ready, okay?"

As Mum leaves the room, questions march in and form an orderly line. I'm not the most patient of people so that line won't stay orderly for long. Mum didn't answer my questions. That means she won't. Not yet anyway. Not until she has all the facts.

*What's happened to Gran?*

Mum's ABM usually means something needs fixing, sorting, defending, paying; that's what she does. Sometimes, I think that's all she does since … well, the less said about 'since' the better. Maybe it's because Mum's a solicitor. Or maybe it's just Mum.

The news *was* bad … *and it was about Gran.*

Tears well.

"Hannah," she calls from the bottom of the stairs,

meaning, 'get a move on'.

I guess I need to flick my switch.

Right.

Tipping the entire contents of my school bag onto my bed – won't be needing any of that – I grab my phone. 3.07 a.m. I tuck it into the side pocket. What else?

Jumper

Socks

Underwear

Kindle

Chargers – most important

3:09 a.m.

Brush

Hat. *Favourite.*

Finally, I stuff deodorant and my lip balm into my bag then thunder down the stairs. I stand at the door, pull my boots on, then begin flicking the latch whilst Mum does a final sweep, double-checking everything is locked and pulling plugs from their sockets. Better to be safe than sorry, she always says. *Is this really happening? Is Gran ...* but I daren't finish that thought.

I open the door ajar, feeling sprays of rain against my face. A flashback from the dream I couldn't remember startles me. *Mum plunging into the black water.* I shudder. Rows of fir trees lining the garden groan and creak against the might of the brutal wind but remain defiant. Years of clustering shore up their leafy ramparts. But tonight's storm is something else. *Never seen it like this. At least that I can remember.* Winter approaching is autumn's warning.

*Argh!*

A low, thick branch of a silver birch tree – one of the ones that Gran planted for me – cracks and falls; bark peeling. It hangs like a flesh wound.

Mum presses her hand onto my shoulder.

"Look at what the storm's doing? That's *my* birch."

She doesn't even acknowledge what I said, just rummages through her handbag, which is filled with Mum's cra- *Huh!* Lightning fills the house then vanishes, but leaves behind a racing heart. *Hate storms.*

"Mum, are you sure you want to drive to Norfolk in *this?*"

She stops rummaging and stares out into the darkness beyond our security light, which gives the sheets of rain a silvery glow.

"No. But we have no choice, love." She pulls one of the huge brollies from the wicker stand and offers it to me. Pulling at the press stud, unravelling the tightly wrapped canopy, Mum gives me a nudge. Finger on trigger, I step out into the storm.

# CHAPTER TWO

## Cold Case

I can't force myself to remember the dream. There's a space where it was that I can't fill. It's only a stone-sized hole, but annoying, like the typical pebble in your shoe scenario. It's strange though because I always remember my dreams. Always.

The storm's watery fists batter the car. Wiper blades slash against the downpour but barely cut through the deluge. *Poor Mum.* Having to drive in this and worry about Gran. We've not seen Gran in six years. And that's six years too many in my opinion. But what does my opinion matter. I'm just a kid. And being relegated to the back seat because of a Mount Vesuvius size pile of files clogging the front footwell right now, really isn't helping. Might as well have a car seat! I pull my green beanie off by its bobble and toss it on the rear shelf.

Gran used to say, "You can't waste time when you're old, especially not as old as me. Hannah, promise me you'll treat each day that comes like it's been dipped in honey. Lap it up."

Some days it's hard to taste the honey.

*I really miss her.* I miss the way she made a perfect slice of buttered toast. I miss her brushing my hair before bedtime. I could list all the little things I miss, but they just add up to one thing. *Her.*

Maybe I'm missing her more because it's October. I know that's a strange thing to say, but it's nearly her birthday. Funny how pain feels worse on those special days. There's nothing *special* about them anymore. Just reminders of happier times. Mum said that they feel like a 'commemoration' to her, even more so since Dad … I guess it's something you just have to get used to.

October 31st. It still makes me laugh that Gran was born on Halloween. Scary. Imagine being born on Halloween? Gran used to tease and say she was really a witch in the disguise of a sweet old grandma who likes liquorice and knitting but I don't believe in witches. And I don't believe I've ever seen Gran knitting. We never missed her birthday until the argument.

A shiver doesn't just skate down my back, it treble-salcos, and it's not because Mum has the air-conditioning belting out to keep her awake. Mum would never discuss the argument she'd had with Gran. 'If you needed to know I would tell you. Case closed,' she would say every single time I'd ask. *Why do I still ask?* I told her every time that I did need to know, but Mum sweeps my persistence away like crumbs on a tablecloth.

Case closed.

*What's the saying they use in crime shows?*

Cold case. That's it! Cold case. Not solved. Just locked away somewhere. But this is a case I just can't leave cold. I have to know.

Now, I know that it's absolutely not the right time to ask, but I can't *not* know. I mean, surely I have a right to know, don't I? And it's not like she can send me to my room and avoid me. We are approaching Lincoln, so there's at least another two hours to Gran's and Mum isn't exactly breaking any speed limits. Not like she would ever actually break the speed limit. 'It's more than my job's worth,' she'd say. And definitely not in *this* weather.

I can't shake this feeling that has pitched a tent in the pit of my stomach. I have to know *why* they fell out and why, right at this minute, the feeling that's pitched is anger.

I guess the phone call has awoken more than I realised. I stare out of the window, yawning deeply. It sends that strange natural trigger straight to Mum. She yawns, then leans forward, concentrating on the cats' eyes that lead the way. I swear the storm's getting worse the further south we travel, or at least that's how it feels. Half the country has been engulfed with floods again and here we are, leaving one floodplain for another. I know now isn't really the best time to ask, but I grip the door handle and begin to pick the lock of the cold case.

"So, it's bad then?" *Please say it's not bad.*

"Can't you tell, Han?"

"Not the road. I mean Gran. You haven't told me anything." *At all … as per usual.*

"Oh." I catch a flicker of concern as she glances back. "I … er, I don't know. Why don't you try to sleep or read?"

I feel sorry for Mum. I mean, having to drive all the way to Norfolk in a storm in the middle of the night whilst worrying about Gran. *What am I doing? Now is not the time.*

"Is Gran dead?"

The words fall from my mouth and smash like glass breaking the silence that has swamped the car. That's the thing with words, you can undo, untie, unfold, but you can't unspeak, can you? I stare into the blackness of the footwell, wishing I could crawl down there and hide.

"What? Of course she's not dead! Hannah, for pity's sake. Do you think if Eleanor had died I'd be in any fit state to drive? I can't believe you've just asked me that." *That hadn't even dawned on me.*

A small cry of relief bursts out from the back of my throat as Mum's words echo … *Eleanor had died … Eleanor had died …*

"Stop calling her that. She's *your* Mum. You wouldn't like it if I started calling you Caroline, would you?" *Hate that.*

"No. I suppose you have a point. I wouldn't." *Then why do it to Gran?*

"You must have some idea if Gran's okay?"

I pull against the seatbelt, but it's not that that's irritating me.

"They didn't say much."

I can't tell if Mum's trying to protect me or avoid the subject. *I just need to know Gran's okay.* My heart flutters like a falcon's wings. I want to get out of the car. To run. But I can't. Trapped in more ways than one. I squint, pressing my face against the rain-lashed glass. Orange glows bleed against the water droplets, the warmness of breath mists the window. *Gran. Please be okay.* I stare at my reflection. Mum always said I'd inherited Gran's almond-shaped eyes, but mine are a greenish-blue rather than a bluish-green, like hers. *Not that I can really tell the difference.*

"Well, what did they say?"

"Just leave it." Mum's tone is as harsh as the rain.

"But what if she's died whilst …"

"Enough, Hannah!" she says smacking her hand on the steering wheel. "She isn't dead!"

Mum loosens her scarf, like it's suddenly difficult to breathe, then tosses her hat into the footwell.

"Well, she must be really ill because there's no way you'd drag us down there at this time of night." And still the trapdoor that is my mouth continues to swing wide open.

"Of course she's really ill."

"But why drag us down there if you despise her so much?"

"Despise? Good Lord, you sound *exactly* like her. She had you eating dictionaries for breakfast when you were four."

"And that's a bad thing?" Mum ignores my reflection in her rear-view mirror. She looks so pale and drained.

"I never said that. And no, of course I don't *despise* her. What a stupid thing to say, Hannah. Why on earth would you …"

Her creased expression stops me in my tracks. Why *would I think she despised her own mother? But, well, she never answered when Gran used to ring and calls her Eleanor, not Mum.*

Maybe I should have gone to sleep or read a book – it's not like my Kindle's battery is flat, but no. Mum had bought it for me last Christmas in the hope I'd start reading more. *It was just more fun when Gran read with me.*

*Why did I open my trap?*

Mum can't hate Gran. Not really. *Do people really ever feel like that?* I couldn't imagine hating Mum. Yeah, she embarrasses the hell out of me sometimes and says no when she could say yes, but hate? *What am I thinking?* As a thick silence settles between us, a thick layer of guilt settles in my stomach.

"I guess it's because we never visit her anymore," I whisper. "We haven't for years. I might have only been seven, Mum,

24

but I do remember."

I swallow the peach-sized lump in my throat. I remember her whitish-brown fluffy hair, which curls in little waves onto her forehead. If I close my eyes and breathe deeply, I can almost smell the lavender and honeysuckle scent she wears every day. I remember how, for a really old lady, she had a vice-like grip whenever she twirled me around in the garden. *I always knew she'd never drop me.* And even how fast she was back then, at her age, too. Gran always caught me when we played tig so I used to believe that people's legs were the last things to get old because Gran was so fast – almost unbelievably so. Gran really was my first best friend. And, let's face it, it's not like I've a load of those to share a selfie with.

The petrol light flashes but Mum only fills the car with silence. She stretches against her tiredness, pulling the seatbelt for a moment's relief, then rubs her neck.

"I just remember you being angry. *Really* angry. And Gran was too. Some huge argument you'd had. And that was the last time we visited. I just don't understand what happened, that's all. I mean, why *were* you so furious with her?"

"Oh Hannah, it was years ago. I don't remember." *Liar.*

"Well, I do."

"That's ridiculous! You can't have been more than five or

six."

*Seriously?* She's done it again; dismissed my thoughts and feelings as if they didn't matter. Adults are infuriating sometimes.

"Like I *just* said, I was *seven* years old."

"Er, what have I told you about that tone? Don't!" Mum inhales deeply. "You know, Hannah-Lou, sometimes I wonder who the mother is in this relationship, young lady. And just so we're clear, it's me. *Not* the one with 'teen' attached to their age group!"

"Sorry, I'm just saying."

"Well don't." Up goes her eyebrow, as usual.

I pick my nails and bite the edge of my thumb until blood – I hate its metallic taste – seeps around my cuticle stinging like mad. I regret it immediately. *'Filthy habit, Hannah,'* Gran would say.

I know I should file the argument away. Just as I begin to actually apologise, Mum says, "Okay, you *really* want to know?"

I hate the way she's just said 'really' but do I want to know?

"Yes. She's my Gran," I say without hesitation. *Why would I ask if I didn't really want to know? Jeez.*

"I will tell you, but then we're done. Okay?"

"Okay."

"You don't get to ask more questions."

"O-kay."

"Elean … your grandmother asked me to do something many years before, which I couldn't do. Then somehow the issue cropped up again the last time we were there for her birthday."

I stay silent. Mum takes a deep breath, then says, "I chose your father over her."

My lungs snatch the air as I fight for breath. *Truth's right hook; didn't see that coming.* Anger clashes with a wall of sadness that has built up in my chest.

*Dad.*

Now him … *him* there was a chance of me hating. Thin rivers of salty tears trickle down my cheeks. Mum reaches for the tissue box from the glove compartment, then pulls four, five, six out and passes them through, squeezing my hand as I take them.

"Don't cry, Han. He's had enough of our tears."

My own anger turns against me, but I can't stop them flowing, like they're betraying me. I brush them away so they don't stain my cheeks.

The divorce was awful. More than awful, it was bloody horrendous. I remember waking in the night so many times to find Mum curled around me. My hair damp from her tears. I hate him for leaving. When Mum told me he was divorcing her, I told her she was wrong, because he was divorcing me, too. And what gets me the most? He didn't deny it. I hoped he would say I was wrong and that I was still his daughter and always would be. But he never did. Not once.

"It was that Halloween when the Decree Absolute came through," Mum whispers as if she can't bear to remind herself of it. It's not something you easily forget. I was just too young to realise that the argument and the divorce were connected. My anger evaporates. A swell of sadness now occupies the space it left. Guilt inches up my chest. I shouldn't have pushed her on it. But then I wonder, should Mum feel guilty, too?

# CHAPTER THREE

## Headlights

We leave Grantham with full bellies and a full tank. Mum has coffee eyes. They're wider than the A1. From her mutterings, she still can't believe the storm is going. *Me neither.* It's as if our journey is on social media and we're being followed. She leans ever closer to the windscreen, navigating the country roads that wind to Attleborough – *to Gran.* Eventually, we pass Swaffham; the roads become rivers in places. Mum slows to a crawl through dips in the road where the water runs deeper.

"Will the car flood?"

"I certainly hope not, but this is Norfolk."

"What?"

"No, no. I'm taking it slowly. And as the saying goes, I know these roads like the back of my hand. Although, I'll never understand that saying. I mean, people don't memorise the back of their hands, do they?" She has a point. Pulling my phone out, I flick the torch on and shine it on the back of Mum's hand. She shakes her head and snuffs a little giggle. Mum's veins look like the branches of an elm tree in winter. I glance at mine, but being smoother makes it difficult to see the veins. They don't protrude like hers do.

I stare out across the flat land of Norfolk, but it's too dark to recognise anywhere. Sunrise is nearly an hour away. Rain still lashes the car like a jockey whipping its thoroughbred. I press the weather app and search our location. Misty but dry. *Perfectly accurate as usual.* I press the icon then hit delete. Let's face it; my big toe's probably more accurate at forecasting the weather.

"Have you missed this place?" Mum asks.

*I have.*

"Have you?" I ask stuffing my phone into my pocket.

"Every damn day."

Mum grew up in Norfolk, but stayed in York after meeting Dad at Uni. After the divorce, she would often ask me if I'd like to move back to Wells where she grew up. 'We can ride the little train to the beach every day, go crabbing on the seafront. Fill our faces with candyfloss from the rock shop,' Mum would say. She'd always wanted to return to Wells and buy one of the cottages on Jolly Sailor Yard. I must admit I was tempted. *Still am.* Maybe we could go while we're here. It might cheer her up.

*Smack!*

"ARGH!"

My shoulder takes the brunt as I slam into the door. *Ow!*

"What's happening?" I scream just as something wallops the car. Not once, but over and over. Tyres scream, a metallic scraping travels down the length of the car. *Mum!*

She yells something back, but I can't hear as we rotate like a waltzer, only this isn't the fun kind of scared.

Are we speeding up?

Shadows of winter-touched trees flash before us.

*Smack!*

"MUM!"

It isn't stopping …

Mum wrestles the steering wheel as the shrill sound of brakes pierces our ears. I grasp the door handle and headrest, knuckles whitening as I cling on. *Why aren't we stopping?* I kick my feet against the back of the chair, bracing myself.

"HOLD TIGHT, HAN!"

We slam into something, which shatters the rear window, spraying glass over me. Shards scratch my cheek. Ow! Bullets of water pummel my body as the storm raids the car. My stomach lurches. Wave upon wave of cries escape, but I can't hear anything now – only a vacuum of silence as I fall under a blanket of darkness.

\*\*\*\*\*\*\*\*\*\*\*\*\*\*\*\*

A voice whistles around my head repeating my name and asks me to wake up. I don't recognise the voice. *Must be a paramedic.* Lights and pain pour into my head like a jug of ice-cold water, forcing my eyes shut. Instead, I begin to feel around for something to grab on to, but then I hear it.

*"Hannah. You must awaken child. I need you."*

Like a python, a voice coils around me. There's no way that's a paramedic. *And it's not Mum.* I swallow hard, but realise I can't actually speak. Or daren't.

The voice hisses, fear snakes down my spine.

*"Wake, Hannah. I command you. You must help me, Hannah. Only you can help me!"*

Fear now laces my eyes shut. I try to block the voice as fluorescent lights flicker and I'm aware of a bright light circling me. *Is it blue?* I hope the light's blue. *Please.*

But then everything fades.

No lights.

No voice.

Just rain.

But the rain isn't clawing me anymore. Instead, it's soft and warm. *How can October rain be warm?* Or is it blood trickling down my face? Blood is warm …

"HANNAH!" screams Mum, jolting me back to here, now.

****************

I open my eyes to feel her releasing the seatbelt and pulling me into her chest. Mum hangs through the gap in the seats, cradling me. *Thank God.* My cheek pulses against her heartbeat. She squeezes me tightly making me wince against the stinging sensation across my face as if the rain is a swarm of bees.

*Ow!*

"Oh sweetheart, you frightened me. You wouldn't wake up," she begins as our bodies gently rock from side to side.

"What happened?"

"Something hit the car. Or the car hit something. I'm not really sure. There's nothing on the road. Just us."

*Nothing?*

"But I saw lights."

"Did you?" She moves me back and examines my face. "It must be the bump," she says stroking my hair, pulling me back close.

I glance over Mum's shoulder to look for other people, vehicles, anything, but she's right. There's nothing.

No ambulance.

No sirens.

No blue flashing lights.

*Where did the lights go?*

Barely a trace of the storm is left – like Mother Nature has left the crime scene and covered her tracks. Only stillness remains. Realising my fist is still balled, I open my hand. Crushed inside is a maple leaf. Slowly, it curls open, like it's discovered sunlight again, revealing a deep shade of red. *Beautiful. But, how is that even possible?*

I cling to Mum, but something feels so wrong.

*Flash.*

I picture the oak tree from my dream, uncurling its branches – just like the maple leaf – ready to catch me, feeling the glow of emerald and gold warm against my face.

*Flash.*

*What's happening to me?*

Suddenly, I wrench myself from Mum, push the door open and throw up. I hang limp over the edge of the seat. I drop the maple leaf onto the glistening tarmac knowing something isn't right.

I know that wasn't Mum's voice calling to me, so whose was it?

# CHAPTER FOUR

## Claw

My body hangs limp.

Fingertips rest against the wet tarmac, which illuminates orange on/off, on/off, like the tick of a clock. Mum's hands wrap around me pulling me back inside the car. Still straddling the gap between front and rear passenger seats as she tries to hold me up. *So dizzy.*

"I'm sorry, Mum."

"Shh. You're okay."

She presses her lips onto my forehead and lingers there holding her breath for a second. Clasping her hands around my head, she checks me over once more and begins a line of questioning I could really do without.

Sunday. Maybe Monday.

September. *Autumn baby.*

Prime Minister? *Who cares!*

Mum thinks I've got signs of concussion. "We'll head for the hospital."

"No. I'm fine, honest. Let's just get to Gran. Please."

"Are you sure?" she asks pulling threads of wet hair from my face.

"Yes, I'm sure. Do you really think Gran's okay?"

"I do. And do you want to know, how I know?" Mum begins counting the freckles on my nose. *She hasn't done that since I was six.* "Because I think your grandmother's given you another one, you know. Eight, nine, ten … yup. Definitely more there, so that couldn't have possibly happened if your grandmother wasn't okay."

"Well, that's absolute proof right there – beyond reasonable doubt – isn't that what you're always checking?"

"It is," she says, a smile beaming from her face.

"Are *you* alright?"

Mum inhales deeply. "Yes. I think so. Counting freckles definitely helps."

Mum squeezes me so tightly. *Feels good.* We stay silent for just a moment letting our body heat spread through each other, although it isn't quite as cold now.

"Okay, I'd better check the car out. I might have to ring the AA."

"Do you want me to come with you?"

"Yes. We shouldn't be sat in the car. It's dangerous, especially on these narrow roads. If you're okay to, get the torches and blankets from the boot. Then stay on the verge whilst I check the tyres."

Almost every scrap of evidence of the storm seems to have vanished. Just a damp road and a damp grass verge. *Storms don't vanish though. They leave a trail, branches ripped from trees, leaves scattered like confetti.*

Feeling a little less queasy, I pull one blanket from the

boot and fling it around my shoulders, tucking a second under my arm. I fumble around for the torches. The boot light isn't working. I actually need a torch to find the torch! Eventually, I feel them both, then holding one between my knees, I smack the other against the palm of my hand. It's flat. Great. I chuck it back into the boot, then try the other.

"Any luck?" Mum calls.

"One's working." I bundle up the other blanket and throw it across to her. As I do, I hold the working torch angled towards the driver's side. Something in its light catches my eye. I feel my legs buckle, but I fight to stay upright.

"MUM!" The scream scorches against the dryness of my throat.

She darts out from under the bonnet to my side and grabs my shoulders. "What? What is it?"

I can't speak. I raise the torch, pointing the beam of light. Mum's gaze follows …

"Oh my God," she says, taking the torch and moving the line of light down the entire length of the car. "Oh. My. God."

We stand wrapped in blankets and silence.

# CHAPTER FIVE

## Caroline
### Silver Fox

"Hannah, get in the car. Right now!"

"Mum, what is it?"

"I don't know. Just get in the car."

*I have to get her out of here.*

I scan the quiet fields and moonlit hedgerows with the torch, trying not to flinch at every one of nature's nocturnal noises. *You forget the sounds of countryside all too quickly living in a large city.* My grip tightens on Hannah's arm. *Something's out there.*

"Ow, Mum," she gasps. I lessen the hold ever so slightly. Hannah pulls her phone from her back pocket and presses the torch app shining it onto the car. I know there is nothing on this Earth that could leave marks that size. Half a dozen claw marks are etched into the paintwork, each with four claw lines pressed in so deep they create ridges. *Not even a grizzly could match marks like that.*

I begin moving Hannah towards the car door. *Inside being the lesser of the two evils.*

*Yip, yip.*

"Huh!"

Startled, I drop the torch. Shards scatter as it shatters. Together we spin round to see a body of black and silver fur, reflecting against the headlights. Its eyes glowing like fire.

"Shh. No sudden movements," I whisper.

Hannah just stands completely transfixed. Her jaw drops.

"Get in," I order through gritted teeth as the rest of the pack appears. Half a dozen at least.

*Yip, yip.*

"But, Mum, what if they're hurt? Shouldn't we check?" *Isn't she afraid?*

Silver foxes are endangered. I've never seen them in the wild, let alone a pack. I know the fox couldn't have clawed our car like that, but something out here has. I scan hedgerows again for any sign of movement. I inhale

HANNAH AND THE HOLLOW TREE

slow and steady. *Mustn't let my nerves show.* How is it that a pack of silver foxes shows up right after our accident? *Could Mum have sent them? Does she know?*

The alpha of the pack pads across tracking the line of our steps, never taking its eyes off Hannah.

"Stay!" I glower, before walking around to the front of the car, unlatching the bonnet, lowering it and then pushing it down.

*Click.*

Suddenly, Hannah darts past me and rushes towards the fox.

"No!"

Grabbing her sleeve, I yank her back. She looks stunned. I open the driver side door and shove her in. She crawls over the handbrake and sits down, rubbing her shin.

"Was that really necessary?"

"Yes!"

"They're just foxes, aren't they?"

"Silver ... silver foxes."

"Really? I didn't even know they existed. I thought you said silver foxes were, like, a good-looking old bloke?

"They're rare. Not endangered. *Yet.*"

"Blokes or foxes?"

*Daft sod.*

"Those foxes couldn't have clawed our car like that," adds

Hannah not daring to take her eyes away from the fox, which is still standing and staring back at us. The remainder of the pack trots forward surrounding it. *Definitely the alpha.*

"No, but something did."

"Look at their eyes!"

The pack move as one, but each pair of eyes catches in the headlights' beams, refracted like a prism; violet and blue, ruby and emerald, amber and bronze. The alpha pauses and sniffs the air.

Suddenly, Hannah yanks at the handle to dive out of the car. I grab her shoulders. "What are you doing?"

"What?"

A sudden dazed look crosses her face.

"What on earth were you going to do, Han?"

"I don't know! I mean ... I just wanted to see if they're hurt."

Hannah's expression is one of utter bewilderment.

"They're so beautiful, Mum. What if we've hit them?"

"We didn't. Something hit us. We can't stay here. It's not safe. I need to speak to your grandmother."

Hannah turns immediately and my heart sinks. She has 'Question Face'. *Why in God's name did I say that!*

I check my keys and go to turn the ignition.

*Zee, zee, zee. Zee, zee, zee.*

"Huh!" we gasp.

41

The vibration sends my heart hurtling into my mouth. Hannah fumbles trying to pull her phone back out from her pocket, then passes it to me.

"It's Joyce," I say swiping right. I change the audio to speaker and rest the phone in my lap.

"Are you two okay, Caroline? I was expecting you by now." I grip the steering wheel letting my head hang for a moment.

"We're okay, Joyce," says Hannah.

"Oh my dear. How lovely to hear your voice. Is your mum there?"

"I'm here, Joyce."

"Caroline. Thank goodness. I was beginning to worry."

"How is … my mum, Joyce?"

"Your mother is stable. Resting," Joyce replies. My spine shudders as relief sweeps through my body. *Hang in there, please Mum. Just hang in there.*

I explain what happened, only this is an edited version of events: foxes in the road, swerving, hitting a tree. I leave out any mention of claw marks. I glance to Hannah and she nods, new version of events noted. I half-smile. She does her 'chin smile', which means those questions have taken aim, ready to fire. *I'd have questions, too, I guess.*

"Oh my goodness!" says Joyce. "I'll send Brian, our ambulance driver out to collect you. He's on call and can be there in a jiffy."

"No. Not necessary. We're fine. We'll be there soon. Don't worry, Joyce. Honestly. Just stay with my mother."

I know it's rude, but I don't wait for Joyce to reply. I close the case and pass Hannah her phone back. Before shoving it in her pocket once more, she checks her notifications. Not like there'd be any at this hour. And this is not something that needs broadcasting.

I register Hannah's expression. I loosen my hair from behind my ears. This time, I'm not fighting tears, but counting the questions I know she'll have. I must speak to Mum because I'll be damned if anyone thinks they can get away with hurting my daughter.

## CHAPTER SIX

# Hannah
## Willows Green

"Honestly, Joyce, we're fine. We're barely five minutes away. Just coming through Attleborough now. Put the kettle on and don't be stingy with the biscuits. Bourbons if you have them."

Joyce had rung again, clearly worried. *Is there something she's not telling us about Gran?*

Mum blasts the heating seeing as the window's shattered across the back seat. Passing through Attleborough, I feel a small swell of relief seeing the town's wooden sign on the green and the flint walls lining the village roads. Maybe we should move to Norfolk like Mum wants. *Maybe we'll have to.*

As we pull into Willows Green Nursing Home, Joyce, waiting with a large umbrella, waves. She dashes across the car park, dodging puddles, pointing to where Mum should park. I'd almost forgotten what she looks like. Her tall, thin frame is topped with brown candyfloss hair. Her face is still soft, her eyes as warm and smiley as they ever were. She doesn't look alarmed, so maybe Gran is okay after all? But nurses are trained to stay calm, aren't they? *How do they do that?*

A gloomy half-light fills the sky. Mum says she feels as

weary as the day looks. Before she climbs out to greet Joyce – who is sheltering under her leaf-shaped green umbrella – Mum whispers, "Remember, co-conspirator now, Han. Stick to the edited version of events."

I nod trying *not* to remember, glancing outside for something, anything that takes my mind off the crash, the claws. *No!* I shake my head.

I stay in the car and study Willows Green. Its size registers with me for the first time. I'd never really paid any attention when I was little. Its weathered stone walls, blackened over the years are unmissable. A stone-carved sign sits above the main entrance. Est.1854 it reads. I remember Miss Bentley teaching us about Victorian workhouses in Year 5. And this one is now Gran's home. Somewhere to be feared by the old and the poor back then.

I wonder if the old fear it now.

*How could Mum leave Gran here?*

*How could anyone leave someone they love here?*

A thin film of drizzle now blankets the windscreen so I push the wiper arm to clear it. I feel a sickness in the pit of my stomach. *Please don't say the storm is coming back.*

*Rain.*

*Wind.*

*Claws.*

*No, dammit!*

I must think of Gran. Mum will summon me any second now, I'm sure. I look to each high-set rectangular window wondering which one Gran spends her days looking out of.

Five…six…seven…eight…ni…

*Ruddy hell!*

The figure of an elderly woman stares down at me from the ninth window.

*Gran?*

I lean forward releasing the seatbelt. Is it really her? It looks like her. I mean, well, the Gran that the seven-year-old me remembers.

I wave.

Her fingers drum against the air, but –

*Huh!*

I feel them …

Clutching my chest, I press my fingertips where hers were.

*How did she do that?*

She's alive.

Gran really is alive – I felt her!

# CHAPTER SEVEN

## The Ninth Window

I fling open the door nearly knocking Joyce sideways, stumbling as I pull my boots back on.

"Look! Up there! Gran's at the window; the ninth one along, see?" *Why didn't Joyce mention Gran was perfectly fine when she spoke to Mum?*

"Oh my dear, that's impossible," Joyce begins, her regal tone soothing. "Eleanor is quite frail. She couldn't possibly be at that window."

*Impossible?* I stare at Joyce who looks sincere enough. My cheeks flush as I begin apologising for hitting her with the car door, but she ushers us inside out of the rain. I glance back up at the windows, but Gran's vanished. *I know it was her.*

My thoughts flit faster than the pages of a book being flicked.

*They don't believe me, but I know what I saw. And felt. Every fingertip!*

The thing is, I swear I smelt her scent too – sweet honeysuckle, soothing lavender. It sounds ridiculous and I guess I know it's impossible. I feel a fog setting in and rub my forehead. Joyce states that I look a 'tad delicate' and promptly guides me to a chair. Mum sits, then presses a kiss onto my forehead. *I don't understand what just happened.*

Forced into waiting with tea and bourbons, I watch Mum bounce her foot, turning each time the ward door swooshes then clicks. Questions march through the thickness of the fog in my head. I play Mum's words over and over. *'I need to speak to your grandmother.'* And I know she spotted my 'Question Face'. I couldn't hide *that* from her. Other than speaking to Gran to know she's okay, why would Mum *need* to talk to her about the claw mark? What would Gran know about it? *Something isn't right.* The feeling that Mum is keeping something from me, yet again, boomerangs back right into my gut. Gran always told me to 'trust my gut'. I used to think she meant so I knew when it was dinnertime, but I get it now. *And I do trust it.*

It's been years since Mum and Gran have actually spoken to each other. *Will they even forgive each other?* Staring at the clock, I watch the seconds-hand tick, tick, tick. It should be daylight by now – 7.52 a.m. – but the day's so grim, I doubt we'll see the sun today.

*Ugh, how much longer?*

I just want to see Gran. I realise that I haven't spoken to Gran for nearly half my life. My heart sinks like the Mary-Rose. The tears are coming. I give in letting them criss-cross down my cheeks. They fall and stain my jumper. My eyes are heavy, but how can I sleep now?

****************

"Gran will be okay won't she?"

"I don't know. I thought we'd be in by now," Mum says squeezing my hand, huffing repeatedly. Mum doesn't do well when she's not being queen bee. This waiting will be killing her. How she hasn't stung someone, I don't know. It's always a near miss on parents' evening, especially. *Hate that.*

The ward doors swoosh and click again. "Caroline, Hannah," Joyce begins softly. "I can take you up now. But, before I do, I must tell you that Eleanor has just suffered another cardiac arrest."

"WHAT? Could this day get any worse?" Mum yells bolting up and dragging me with her, but Joyce blocks her wagging her finger as if Mum's a five-year-old or something. Before Mum has chance to speak, Joyce takes her hand clasping both of her own around it.

"Everything will be okay, Caroline. Just calm down. I know it's pointless telling you not to worry, but she is in good hands. I think you know that."

*What did she mean by that?*

Joyce and Mum exchange a look that makes my stomach somersault like before. *I don't like this.* I can't describe it, but it's like when two people do that thing of sharing a private joke – only they know – something to the exclusion of all others. Once again, it's me being excluded.

"I *need* to speak to my mother, Joyce."

"We have been able to stabilise her again, but she is very weak, Caroline," Joyce begins but tilts her head towards me. "She will just look like she's sleeping, okay, Hannah?"

I nod as she continues. "There are machines in there that help us monitor her condition. Don't be alarmed by what you see or hear. It is standard procedure and there to make her more comfortable."

Numbness grips my legs as we begin walking through the gloom-shrouded place where Mum left Gran. As we move down the corridor, I notice my reflection in the shine of the bottle green tiles, trailing my fingertips across their smoothness.

"Han, slow down a little."

But I can't.

How is it possible that Gran has nearly died again? My footsteps quicken. *Where are all the soddin' doctors? What hit our car?* This just doesn't make sense, but then nothing about today does. *Something* had hit the car. Something with claws. Massive claws. And it *was* Gran I'd seen at the window. I'd bet my life on it. There has to be a logical explanation, but if there is, I have no idea what.

*Run.*

My stomach churns responding to that hospital stench

which I am forced to inhale. Bleach lingers in the air. I cover my mouth. I've already been sick once today.

*Run.*

"Hannah, slow down. Wait for us," Mum calls. But my legs are eager. I feel my calves tense. I rush forwards.

"HANNAH!" Her tone halts me immediately, never mind the volume, which ricochets off the walls. Gentle Joyce is not so gentle all of a sudden. She walks up to me with one of those perma-smiles that people use like masks.

"You don't know where you're going, Hannah. Not the old room, like before."

*Yes I do. Third floor. Nine windows. Nine doors.*

Joyce's green eyes flash and narrow. "Hmm, did you … *say* something my dear?"

I cough trying to catch my breath to speak. *Has Joyce just read my mi … as if, you idiot. Get a grip! Of course she can't read minds.* Joyce turns on her heels and leads us up to Gran's room. Pausing at Gran's door, she rests her hand on the brass handle, before turning back to us. She looks to Mum, then me.

"Now, Hannah, I don't want you to worry about what you see," Joyce's serene tone has returned, but in truth I am only half listening. I can't get her expression off my mind. That flash in her eyes. It must have been the light bouncing off tiles, or something. *Pay attention.* Eventually,

51

I tune into what she is actually saying, nod, and remember I didn't finish apologising for hitting her with the car door.

"I hope I didn't hurt you, Joyce."

"Not at all and thank you dear for your apology," she replies as she steps into the room. Mum follows, her firm grip pulls me in behind her. A sudden defiance rises in me taking me by surprise. *I know Gran was at that window. She's fine. I know she's fine.*

I can't see Gran in the bed yet, but I hear the rattle of her chest as she struggles for air.

Something on the left catches my eye.

Petals are falling.

They fall by the dozen from the bedside cabinet.

Dead petals. Grey.

*Oh my God.*

I take one step forwards, my eyes tracking the stream of petals and notice Gran's arm. Thin. Frail. Her bony fingers clutching the stems of what were once white and red roses. They crumble into ash and drift downward.

Beep … beep … beep.

Her body is still.

Beep … beep … beep …

# CHAPTER EIGHT

## The Voice

"THAT'S IMPOSSIBLE!" The words explode out as anger seizes me and won't let go.

"Hannah!" gasps Mum.

"But Gran *was* at the window. I'm not lying. I am not a liar, Mum. Gran, wake up! Please, wake up!" I want to take her hand, but something stops me. I stare at the ashes on the floor.

"Hannah, listen to me," begins Joyce, moving round the bed. "Look at your grandmother."

But I can't see *her*. Only wires and machines and crisp white sheets. The mask covers her face. *I can't bear this.*

"Look at the windows, Hannah. Look how high they are. Are you telling me that Eleanor could reach up there?" she says pointing upwards. The windows must be six foot from the floor, at least. Gran couldn't have even peered over the ledge if she'd been on her tiptoes. *But how did I see her then? It was Gran. I know it was.*

Beep. Beep. Beeeep …

Huh!

Before I can reply, Joyce dashes forward hitting a red button on the wall. Mum turns and pales.

"Mum!" She cries clutching Gran's hand. "Please, no, Mum. I'm sorry! Don't leave me. Don't you dare leave me!"

Another nurse rushes into the room, picks up the control whilst Joyce begins compressions. The motorised bed buzzes as it levels out. My heart thrums faster than a hummingbird's wings. *Don't hurt her!* Somehow I am moving backwards. I hit the cream wall, feeling its coldness under my fingertips.

"Stop it! Stop it! STOP IT!" I cover my face, but peer through lashes and watch the nurse's compressions. "You're hurting her!"

*Don't. Don't hurt Gran.*

"Caroline, move back and let us work. See to your daughter. Caroline, look at me!" Joyce clicks her fingers in front of Mum's face. "Your daughter *needs* you!"

Mum's arms envelop me. Her heart pounds through her chest as she struggles to catch her own breath.

"It's okay, Hannah. It's okay. Gran will be fine, I promise. Come with me, come on." I want to believe her, but the machines are telling a different story.

She pulls me close. Shields me, but it's too late. Once seen never forgotten. Scarred. And the thing with scars is, they fade but never vanish. As Mum begins to usher me out of the room, everything slows. Echoes of Joyce's voice, the machines and Mum's words of comfort all become a babbling mess. Each compression on Gran's chest, each beep of the monitor, each stroke of Mum's hand, all melt into each other.

I feel dizzy.

Then I hear it.

And all the confusion I feel and see blows away like cascades of leaves waltzing in a warm breeze.

"Hannah."

The voice echoes. It is not the voice from the car, so I dare myself to look up.

And there, a phantom in white.

Gran.

# CHAPTER NINE

## Eleanor
### Reaction

Hannah's mouth falls open. She looks across to where my resting body lies then back at me. Her eyes never meet mine. *She thinks I'm dead.* She rips herself from Caroline's grip and launches herself toward the door. With power that she has yet to fathom, she flings it open. Thankfully, Caroline's reaction is quick, shielding her face as the panes shatter. Hannah's reaction is not what I expected, but then what on earth did I expect?

"Hannah?" screams Caroline, but our darling girl flees. Disregarding the shattered glass, Caroline runs to the door. "Hannah, come back!"

Caroline glances to my body, but then runs from the room. And she is quick. I am drenched in guilt; mortified by Hannah's reaction. Surging after them, I catch an emerald glimpse of my soul reflected in the tiles but I look away. *What a fool! What a ruddy fool!* How is it only now that I comprehend what I actually look like to my granddaughter? Did I truly think she would rush to me in this ghost-like form and seek comfort? *What have I done?* I … I of all people, have now endangered them. *Why didn't I listen to Joyce!* I have been so consumed by the news from Galtonia that haste has consumed me.

Reaching the staircase, Caroline grips the mahogany rail and practically throws herself over it screaming her daughter's name. I want to drown myself in her anguish, but self-loathing will have to wait. Pushing forward, I arrive at Caroline's side to see the briefest glimpse of Hannah's hand sliding down the railing immediately beneath us. Caroline kicks off her shoes, taking the stairs two at a time in her desperation to close the gulf between herself and Hannah. *I wonder if she feels my presence.* The further we descend, the further my guilt stretches out before me. Air escapes me as I feel my strength ebb away. I just don't have the energy like I once did but that's something I can lament later.

Caroline closes the gap, leaving me a little way behind.

Hannah hits the last step, then tears across the reception, dodging an array of furnishings. Caroline is close. She reaches out just far enough, grabbing Hannah's jumper and forces her daughter to a standstill. Caroline doesn't let go, the jumper twisting in her hands until she can grab hold of Hannah's arm.

"What on earth is the matter, Hannah?" Caroline pants, pulling her close.

"Let me go. Let me go. It's too late. We're too l …"

Hannah's eyes widen. I feel her horror pierce me. *She's so scared.* All she sees is a spectre. All I feel is a fool.

"Hannah, wait. Listen to me!" I call out. *She thinks I'm*

*dead.*

Caroline turns. "What are you looking at, Hannah? What is it?"

But Hannah seizes the moment, yanks herself free and darts for the revolving doors, smashing through a grief-stricken couple. I flash forward shimmering through the glass. *Cold, as always.* A terrific screech fills the car park as tyres sing in agony clawing at the wet tarmac.

"HANNAH!" The guttural scream from deep within Caroline almost renders me catatonic. Instead, I fight hard, pushing my soul as far as I can, sweeping directly beneath my granddaughter, but it isn't enough. Caroline's screams ring out as the car clips us and we hurtle across the bonnet of another. I twist my form protectively. Am I too late? We smack against the bumper of a van, landing heavily. I instantly smell the blood now trickling down her temple.

*What have I done?*

*No! This cannot be.*

I listen momentarily for her pulse …

*Yes. There!*

With a whisper, I remove the veil from Caroline's mind that has cloaked my presence. I gather myself.

"Caroline, quickly! Help me," I call.

She has never seen me in spirit form before, but I can't wait for her to snap herself out of shock. Cradling Hannah's head, I scoop her up and glide towards Caroline.

"Mum?" Colour drains from her.

"Take her, Caroline. I am weak. I cannot sustain this for very much longer. HERE, CAROLINE!"

But her knees buckle and as she lands in a pool of rain, its spray makes me shiver. I have now only one option. I place Hannah across Caroline's collapsed body.

My spirit flickers and flashes like a drained battery.

*I just need a moment more.*

Erratically, I push upwards and aim for the ninth window. I shimmer through the chilling glass, spiralling down. I smash into my corpse-like body; the sheet pluming as I return to my corporeal form.

The searing pain in my chest takes my breath away. My eyes widen. "Help my girls!"

Joyce's thoughts flash into my mind. *"Where?"*

*"The car park!"*

With that, Joyce pulls her hand from her pocket and blows a tiny dose of lavender into Nurse Alice's face. She falls fast, but Joyce catches her and drags her into that horrendous porta chair I am carted around in. A few hours' sleep will do Alice the world of good. Shifts are far too long in this place.

Joyce vanishes.

My bones sink into the soft mattress as I rub my chest against the excruciating pain. That's the thing with astral projection, when you're wired to machines it sounds exactly like a heart attack. The physical pain from Alice's compressions is tolerable, just about, but the anguish I have caused the two most precious beings in my world, now that is unbearable. *Eleanor Walsingham you old fool!*

Entering Hannah's sub-conscious is not something I do with ease, but my own stupidity leaves me no choice. The warning from Galtonia must be heeded. I have to explain exactly what is happening. I must prepare Hannah for what is to come and this most precarious of situations demands it.

My internal hazard warning light flashes indicating the blood sugar drop. A sideways glance fills me with relief. *Oh, Joyce! What would I do without you my friend?* Behind the empty yellow vase is a small pink Cyclamen in full bloom. Beautiful in its simplicity. I feel a pinch of remorse as I stretch out clasping its velvety leaves and plush petals. The scent is delicate. Closing my eyes and breathing deeply, I welcome the freshness as it pulses through my veins. The

Cyclamen crumbles through my fingers, leaving nothing but ash.

Gaia needs us ... needs the Potential ... needs Hannah.

# CHAPTER TEN

# Hannah
## The Dream Between

The sand is soft under my feet. Soft and warm. I love running on beaches. Especially this one. Holkham's golden carpet stretches for miles and miles. I slow to dodge pools from the low tide and watch an avocet dip its thin curved beak under water. *Perhaps it's thirsty.*

The crisp sea air is welcome after battling the fumes of city living. *I think Mum's right, we should move here.*

My feet seep into the damp sand. Pulling them free, I continue running, heading for the woodland, inhaling its pine scent. Taking one of the fenced paths, the sand becomes finer, making it harder to walk in, but I push through avoiding pieces of flint and bark. Resting on a felled pine tree, I dust my feet off then pull on my Converse.

I walk until dusk settles in.

*Maybe I should text Mum.*

I pat my denim shorts for my phone, but it's gone.

*Oh my God!*

With light fading fast, I run back to the tree trunk and pat the floor around where I sat. No luck.

*I'll never find it now!*

I continue retracing my steps. Maybe as notifications arrive, I'll see it light up.

*I must get back to the beach.*

It takes just a few minutes before I'm crossing the wooden path. I look up towards the line of huts searching for anyone that could ring my number for me, but there's no one. It's deserted. Luckily, the tide hasn't turned yet so it won't get washed away.

I head back towards the main entrance at Lady Anne's Drive where I started and notice a figure in the distance.

*Yes! Someone at last.*

I jog towards them, waving and calling to get their attention. I think it's a girl. Maybe my age.

*She'll definitely have a mobile.*

"Excuse me, can you help? I've lost my phone. Could I ring my number?"

The girl doesn't turn, just stares out at the sea so I jog right next to her and tap her shoulder.

*Hmm, same perfume.*

"Excuse me?"

As she turns, my entire body shudders like I'm being electrocuted.

"How can you … I don't understand."

"What don't you understand?" she says.

"But … you're me."

"Well, of course."

*Maybe I should be afraid but I'm not. Freaked out, yes. But not afraid.*

I stand in front of myself, same almond-shaped eyes, only hers glow like sapphires and emeralds. Same pale skin, but hers shimmers with a hint of cucumber green. Same fawn-coloured freckles across her nose. But through her hair are vines of ivy and sprigs of holly berries. Her cheeks are flushed and she smiles at me.

*I'm smiling at myself.*

From her huge green gown, the other Hannah pulls out my phone.

"I think this is what you're looking for."

"Thank you."

"You're welcome."

"This can't be real. I must be dreaming."

"Of course you're dreaming, but that doesn't make it any less real."

"Dreams aren't real, though," I say.

"You'll see, soon enough."

From somewhere in the sky, the avocet glides down and lands upon my ... her shoulder. The other Hannah holds out the palm of her hand filled with little pieces of crustaceans.

"Now, Hannah, it's time to wake."

"But what if I don't want to."

"You have to. Someone's waiting for you. And you can never be me if you don't wake up."

"Am I meant to be you?"

"I hope so."

"Will I remember this?"

"Maybe. Later, I think. Now, wake up Hannah."

"Bye."

"Goodbye."

*Flash!*

His greying face shielded against the impact ... I skim

the car.

*Flash!*

Something pushes me up. Ow!

*Flash!*

"Wake up, Hannah. Wake up."

# CHAPTER ELEVEN
## Control

I don't know how long I've laid here for, but my entire body refuses to stop trembling, even as the sobs stutter and fade. Then the flashes come, splintering the blackness, bursting through the cracks. Eyes still closed, but I see it. See what happened. I can't tell if it's the tyres screaming or me. The driver's face hanging in horror. He couldn't have stopped what happened next. My body didn't register the car or the pain. It must have been instant. He will remember my face and I will remember his for all eternity.

I open my eyes, but I'm blinded by darkness. And this … this is where I'm to spend eternity?

*Have I done something so bad?*

Do I deserve this?

*I can't breathe.*

My lungs demand air.

"MUM!"

*Do something!* I don't know if I'm pleading with myself or Mum, but I realise I have to do something. I can't wish myself out of this. I'm not waking from a dream. This isn't what I expected heaven to be like. In fact, I am certain it isn't heaven at all. I don't think Mum is with me, but I call out to her anyway. She doesn't answer, and that's good, I guess because she's probably still alive, whilst I, on the other hand, am –

*Breathe.*

I should be at home in York, in my bed, warm, safe.

*Breathe.*

Instead, I'm in a different county and …

*Breathe.*

If it's not true … but what other explanation can there be?

Blackness surrounds me, thick and velvety, it draws in. I can't swallow, but I press my fingers to my lips to check I'm still breathing. My eyes haven't adjusted as there's nothing to adjust to. No daylight, no fluorescent strobes, no Kindle glow for bedside reading.

"Hello? Mum? Anybody?"

"Shh, Hannah. You are perfectly safe."

"Mum, is that you? I can't see you."

I know this voice.

"You are safe, Hannah."

"Where are you?"

"Close. Don't worry my dear."

But that's the first thing I do as I realise …

*It isn't Mum.*

*It isn't my mum.*

And like a tap, more memories drip into my mind.

*Her voice.*

*The floating gown.*
*Frantic footsteps.*
*My frantic footsteps.*
*Doors revolving.*
*Rain.*
*Car.*
*Driver.*
*Gran!*

"STAY AWAY FROM ME!"

My heart flutters, legs twitch. *I've got to get out of here.* But where is 'here'?

"You're perfectly safe here my darling."

"Safe? Yeah, right! Where's my mum?" I scramble around trying to feel for something, anything I can hold on to. All I feel is a carpet of grass.

"Calm down, Hannah. Please. You don't have to be alarmed like this."

"Why can't I see anything?"

A frosting of fear begins to chill my blood, rising through my legs making them stiffen, but just as I feel it begin to swallow me, it stops. Like the fear is being rinsed away. In its place, a soothing haze of calm floats down through my hair and onto my shoulders. I inhale lavender and sweet honeysuckle. *Gran.* Seconds ago I felt petrified, but now I feel a warmness simmering under my skin. *How is that possible?*

"I am here, Hannah. Look up, sweetheart," she says.

"It's pitch black."

"Humour an old lady."

*A dead old lady more like.*

I tilt my head up, reach out and feel nothing but stupid as my hand pushes against the velvety blackness once more.

"There's nothing."

"You didn't even try." Her tone is firm.

I feel a sudden surge of anger, but once more it drains to a trickle then vanishes. "I don't want to try. Please. I just want Mum."

"I sense your fear, your anger and uncertainty, Hannah. But believe me when I tell you, you have nothing, *nothing* to be afraid of."

I was afraid, but I didn't know what scared me more – Gran's ghost or being dead. *It's Gran, you idiot. She's your grandmother.*

"Just breathe and try once more, Hannah."

And so I do as she asks and the very second I do, a candle-shaped light appears, then another and another. Not close enough to touch, but I reach out craving their light like a sugar fix as they form a circle around me. Something flutters past my face. Instinctively, I swipe at its waspish feel, but then more of them flutter past my face. In the glow of the light, I see a million flecks of rose gold petals begin falling like confetti. I stand, cupping them. *Beautiful.*

"Gran."

"Yes, dearest?"

"Are you doing that?"

"No. It's Dorothy Jenkins in room 302."

"You're not funny, Gran."

"Funny, no. Sarcastic, yes."

A breathy laugh escapes. Her voice is like warm tea on a cold day.

"Gran?"

"Yes, dear."

"*How* are you doing that?"

"The confetti? Ah, just a little parlour trick, nothing more."

"I didn't mean the confetti."

"I know. You are a quick study, aren't you?"

"So? How are you controlling my feelings then?"

# CHAPTER TWELVE

## Forgiveness

I figure it out because Mum likes to remind me how much of a hothead (something I get from Dad's side of the family apparently) I can be. I mean, how else could I leapfrog from fear and anger to cupping confetti like the five-year-old version of me at Aunt Janette's wedding?

"You owe me an answer, Gran. I can't tell which feelings are mine and which are yours?"

"Oh, they're all yours sweetheart. You have such calm energy inside you, as well as *all* the others I am, detecting. I just focused on that and, well, magnified it. I put you through hell back there and for scaring you, Hannah, I am truly sorry. Our reunion didn't work out quite how I hoped it would."

"And was that you in the car? When we crashed?"

"No, not exactly. And not whilst you were in the car, but we will discuss that later, and with your mother too."

*Someone else then, but who?*

The thought curdles my stomach. Have I dreamt it? I feel so unsure of everything to the point of dizziness. My legs quiver so I sit back down on a floor I cannot see.

I hesitate over a question, but can't ask it, so instead say, "How is that even possible, Gran? I mean, controlling people's feelings. That's like Sci-Fi or something."

"I'll opt for 'or something' at the moment. And, well, it's all just a matter of energy, really. It is known as ethereal manipulation, if you want me to be a bit more 'Sci' about it."

"You still haven't told me where Mum is or why I can't see you."

"There is a part of you, albeit small, that is unsure of me and I understand your feelings completely, Hannah."

As Gran begins speaking, I search the room trying to track the sound of her voice as it moves against the blackness.

"That uncertainty is creating a sort of energy barrier between us. You are in one place. I am in another. And because of the barrier we can't fully connect."

It wasn't the answer I was expecting. I'm sort of relieved by it. Twice I've asked for an answer and been given the truth, not really knowing if I could handle the truth.

"I guess it's a form of protection you're secreting," adds Gran.

"Secreting? Yuck! Like sweat?"

"Goodness, no."

From the army of questions that march towards me, one takes aim.

"When did you die?"

*I really need to learn to shut up.*

"I'm not dead, Hannah," she chuckles. "Far from it."

*So it's me who's dead.*

Before I drown in an ocean of panic, the scent of honeysuckle kissed lavender puffs out like Mum's AirWick Freshmatic, which I inhale deeply.

Gran's words echo as my breathing settles. 'Far from it.'

"But, wait. The machines. Those noises they make when people … you know … die. They flat-line. Joyce told us you'd had a heart attack."

"I am sorry for lying to you about that. Being a nursing home, it was a matter of keeping up a pretence. The machines made it sound like I was having a heart attack, but that wasn't the case. I will explain more, my dear, but we have very little time, so we must focus on why we are here. I will speak truthfully to you."

Surely, there's only a certain amount of 'truth' that a person can stomach in one day. I was pretty certain I had had my fill, but no, another course was being served and this one I hadn't ordered.

"You've just worked out that I have a gift. I can manipulate people's emotions. Well, I have a few more, too. It is not just people's emotions, but nature, energy and it is something you …" Gran's words trail away.

If I could see her face now, it would be the calculation one. The one that Mum does. The one that I do.

"I have the power to affect emotions because I am an Empath. That's what you have just experienced. And earlier,

74

when you fled the room – which I take full responsibility for – that was astral projection."

"I've heard of that in stories and stuff."

"It takes an immense amount of energy to split one's soul from their body."

And like a freight train the truth just keeps coming.

"Before I tell you anything further, Hannah, I need you to listen to me very carefully."

*Do I have a choice? All I know is that I should be freaking out right now, what with being dead an' all, but Gran, the Empath, isn't letting me, which I suppose is kinda cool and, in a way, I'm grateful for.*

"I want your forgiveness, Hannah. I can feel your hurt and I am truly sorry I abandoned you all these years. I separated myself from you and Caroline because of my own pride. It is perhaps my biggest regret."

Tears prick, then dribble down my cheeks and I can't stop them.

"Please don't cry, my darling," Gran says, her voice soothing. I feel a feather-light touch of calmness settle over me once more.

"Can … can you *see* me?" I ask.

"I can, yes."

I should be surprised, but I'm getting used to it. After all, I did think Gran was a ghost.

"We all have light inside us, Hannah and we all have darkness too. In most cases, light is predominant, but that energy can shift. Do you understand?"

"I think so."

"If you truly believe in someone Hannah, you will always see their light, their true self. You're still uncertain so you're trying to see me using your eyes and not your heart."

*That sounds ridiculous. Who sees with their heart?*

"Can you see me now?" I ask.

"Yes. Do something so I can prove it to you."

The image of Gran up at the ninth window returns – drumming her fingers in the air – so I do that. Exactly like she did, but twice.

"I only did it once at the window."

*What!*

"How … how is that possible?"

"If I am honest, Hannah, I don't know the exact science behind that one. All I know is that we are family. You are my flesh and blood, a gift so precious. That is the only way I can think to explain it."

I sort of understand what Gran means about me being a gift, but I suppose all grandparents feel like that. And Gran can see me. Really see me.

Now, I feel more confused than ever. It's weird, but I feel ashamed too, like it is my fault that I can't see her. Like

76

there is something wrong with me. And then the softness of Gran's hand lifts my chin.

"Always hold your head high."

With Gran so close, her scent lingers between us.

"Are you controlling my feelings again?"

"No. It's just my perfume this time, sweetheart."

She takes my hands and just like Mum does, presses a kiss onto my forehead. There's been a lot of that today. All the panic about Gran has been for nothing. Now I just feel sick because I'm dead.

Suddenly, a tiny light appears. "Do you see it, Hannah?"

"Yes."

I fix my eyes on its brightness and warmth. It reminds me of Tinkerbell, although it moves slower than she does. It begins to grow, circling round and round, inching closer to me. As it does, it reveals more and more; darkness retreats like a fallen army. Gran stands just in front of me, or maybe she's floating. Yes, I like the idea that she's floating. I've missed that enormous smile of hers. Gran is shrouded in a peach-coloured glow, her gown fluttering around her ankles.

"You know, Hannah, you do have a beautiful way of expressing yourself sometimes my dear girl."

"Mum says I get that from you."

"It's all those books you read. Nothing wrong with

dictionaries for breakfast, either. I do hope you're still a bookworm."

Guilt twangs like a rubber band in my gut.

"Not quite as much," I admit.

"Hmm, so you're cheating on books with all this damn technology, is that it?"

"A bit. I mean … I do have a Kindle though. And it's loaded with books."

"I have absolutely no idea what you just said," Gran says, her eyebrow practically rising to her hairline.

The little orb of light lingers in the air close to my cheek, its glow warm. In one gentle swift motion the light sweeps over me. Maybe I was on my way to heaven after all and Gran was taking me there. *Maybe she's my guardian angel now.*

"Oh, that's very sweet of you. I've never been called an angel," her smile widens.

"You're definitely a mind reader then?"

Gran's eyes sparkle.

"And by the way, Hannah, you are most certainly *not* dead."

# CHAPTER THIRTEEN

# Joyce
## Potion

Fortunately, the rain is easing and the lifting clouds allow the tiniest crack of sunlight through. I let the curtains fall not wanting any hint of daylight to wake Caroline, who has slept for nearly three hours; no concussion, merely exhaustion.

I did warn Eleanor that her idea on how to speak with her granddaughter without Caroline knowing about it was, at best, foolish. But that stubbornness won through all rational attempts to choose another means by which to contact her. I offered to purchase a mobile phone for her but Eleanor can't resist the theatrics!

Caroline stirs ever so slightly so I move closer, and taking the pipette lean over to drop another small dose of sleeping potion onto her lips, but the bottle flies from my hands as she shoves me to the floor.

"What on earth do you think you're playing at?"

Caroline flings back the covers and bolts up – weight shifting from one foot to the next – predatory. She screams at me again and demands to know where Eleanor has taken Hannah, but Eleanor needs more time, something Caroline will not allow.

"Did you drug me, Joyce?"

"No. You passed out," I reply pulling myself up before sidestepping to block her only exit.

"Don't lie to me! Move away from the door and let me past."

"I can't do that. You have to trust your mother, Caroline."

"I don't trust anybody, especially not her where my daughter is concerned. I know what she wants. Now I'm telling you, Joyce. Get out of my way."

"No, Caroline. I am under orders to keep you here."

And with that, she lunges at me. I move aside and blow a concentration of lavender into her face. Caroline sways for a moment, coughing and wheezing. I catch her as she falls and we crumple to the ground. *Rest, Caroline. You're going to need it.* Her eyes dilate and glaze as the shock within ebbs away.

*"Eleanor, get a damn move on!"*

# CHAPTER FOURTEEN

# Hannah
## The High Council of Earth

I'm not dead.

It takes a while for it to sink in. I say it over and over to myself, hardly daring to believe it.

Gran reaches into her pocket and takes out what looks like a tiny little flower, blood-orange in colour. Cupping it, she covers it in warm breath before releasing it out across the room, creating a radiance around us. "What is that?"

"Fire flower. We need a touch more light in here."

*Cool.*

"Touch it."

"Won't it burn me?"

"Oh goodness, no."

The fire flower hovers over my head like a drone. I tap it.

"Two of them!"

"Keep tapping, Hannah."

With each tap I hear a minute giggle like I've tickled it. Each duplicate so I keep tapping until dozens cloud above us creating little rainbow-filled spheres of light.

"They're so beautiful. How do they do that?"

"Oh, I don't know. How do you split genes or atoms? And, fire flowers don't just allow anyone to touch them you know."

"What do you mean?"

Gran smiles, in a sort of 'you'll find out later' kind of way. I glance around the room.

"So, where exactly are we?"

Gran explains that we are in an antechamber. *I sort of know what that means.* It's not what I was expecting, but then what was I expecting. Costa? It's a near-perfect symmetrical room, with limestone walls and thick angular pillars, creating two curving rows of arches. Eight huge candles light the room, the kind you only see in cathedrals, all encased in iron and attached to the chamber's walls. Underneath each candle are four sculptures of strange creatures; two of which have parts of animals, like eagles' wings and lions' tails. The remaining two look mythical, all sabre-teeth and giant scales and clawed-toes on human-like legs.

*What is this place?*

In the centre of the room, raised on a stone platform, and between eight of the pillars, sits a large, circular oak table. I stand on tiptoes to see what's glinting against the candles' light. From its centre twists rope-like lines of gold, etched deep into the table that stretch out to its edges. Placed around the table are four enormous empty thrones, made of huge plinths of different woods.

*Is this some sort of castle?*

What looks like ash or maple, so light in colour, weaves with branches of walnut that wrap around the legs and arms of all four thrones. Each one is a large slab of combined oak and mahogany, which fans out, its edges jagged. I guess spending hours in Dad's workshop learning about wood and stuff, sort of stuck.

*I miss that.*

Binding parts of the plinths together are brackets and buckles of iron and copper. Directly behind each of the four thrones, sits one of the eight pillars in the room. Distinguishing those four, are the letters N, E, S, W etched into them. *Hmm, Never. Eat. Shredded. Wheat.* Directions, I'm guessing.

"But *where* exactly are we, Gran?"

"And *when*, dearest, *when*, but we'll get to that later. A smidgen of patience, please."

Gran's response is strange. But then, the whole day hasn't exactly been normal, has it? Gran continues, and I can't help but detect that truthful tone of hers, which is now putting my gut on high alert. It begins to churn. And, you know what you get when you're ill? Penicillin. I think truth is like Penicillin. No matter how bad it tastes, sometimes, you've just got to swallow it, whether you want to or not.

"Hannah," says Gran patiently. "You are lying in a bed, and I am now next to you on a chair. We are both asleep.

I have the gift of projection, in many forms, and it allows me to enter anyone's sub-conscious mind. I have done this now, with you, in order to bring you to this place and explain why I sent for you and your mother."

"WHAT?" I choke on the word in disbelief.

"I sense anger surfacing, Hannah. You need to learn to control that, my dear. It will get you into trouble one of these days."

*Gran is in my head? Or, her mind is in my mind. That's crazy!*

Anger comes up for air, but my body feels like it's being dragged under the currents; gravity refuses to let me breathe. I half expect Gran to waft her hand over me to control my emotions, but she doesn't. "It's up to you to control it now, not me." I take in four, five, six breaths.

"Are you telling me you're in my head?"

"Your subconscious, yes. Precisely. After I scared you half to death, which was not my intention whatsoever, of course, well, you ran. And rather fast, too. Do you remember?"

"Yeah, I ... I ..." *Breathe, breathe.* "I ran out to find our car."

"Well, you *did* find a car, my dear, but, not the one you were aiming for, shall we say. I had only just enough strength to lift you above the car that was a whisker away from hitting you. I'm afraid I had to push you out of the way to ensure your safety."

Gran pauses to brush a curl away from her eye, but catches a tear instead. "But in doing so, my darling, in such a desperate moment as that, I pushed you too hard. You flew up, over that car and landed much too heavily on the bonnet of another car. I couldn't reach you in time, you slid down, hitting your head."

Her tears fall and bleed into the corners of her mouth. Taking the edge of one sleeve, she dabs her face. I have never seen my grandmother cry. How can I be angry with her now? It was her fault that I ran, but she couldn't have known about the car. Guilt paints itself across her face, which makes me uneasy.

"I can bring you round very quickly, but … but I cannot do that right now, my dear, because there is an important reason for us being here. We have much more to get through and not a lot of time."

*I can't do this. I just can't.*

"Gran, please get out of my head. I don't want to get through more. If what you've told me is true, then I'm begging you to wake me up. Please, I want Mum. I just want to see my mum."

For a moment, it looks like Gran is going to wake me up, but then she glances around the chamber, almost as if she is expecting someone, and her tone changes.

"I cannot do that. Your mother is asleep. Joyce is taking

care of her."

"Does that mean Joyce knows all this?"

"Yes."

"Knows about what you can do? Where you are now?"

"Yes, everything. She is a sister spirit, like me in many ways." Gran grips my shoulders. "Hannah, dearest. I want you to understand that you are perfectly safe. And do you think I would be so calm if something serious had happened to my daughter or to you?" *She sounds just like Mum.*

"I swear that as long as I am breathing, nothing ... *nothing* Hannah will happen to you."

"Are you still breathing? I mean, your body, you were ... the nurses were ..."

"Yes. I am still breathing. The truth is I was never in any danger of dying. It was astral projection, remember? But being hooked up to machines, makes it sounds like heart failure I am afraid. It is a pretence that has been necessary."

*Gran's been pretending to be ill?*

"But why?"

"Well, it's widely accepted that the earth has been suffering and for some time, now. And it's only getting worse. Floods, hurricanes, droughts, wild fires. This year alone more creatures have been listed as extinct than in any previous year on record. Orangutans, gone. Black rhinos, gone. Hawksbill turtles, gone. Yet we continue to multiply."

"Climate change."

"Yes."

"But what does that have to do with you pretending to be ill?"

"Well, because of our family history …"

Gran pauses, looking utterly lost for a moment.

"Are you okay?"

She swallows and nods. "The best way to begin to explain is to show you."

Gran offers her hand. I press my palm against hers, our fingers interlock.

*Crack!*

I flinch, shielding my face, wincing against the sudden brightness. It fades, quickly leaving an oval-shaped hole like a hollow in a storm beaten tree. It's as if the hand of a seamstress has continued cutting well past the end of her cloth and snipped away the fabric of the world. The cut of the hollow is clean, no fraying edges. I want to reach out, trace my fingers along the cut and feel beyond it, but Gran's grip turns her knuckles white. Through the hollow I can see a room which is bizarrely, almost identical to the one we are standing in. The same limestone walls look brighter though, like lickable sticky syrup. I can't imagine limestone tastes of lime, though.

*Vrump. Vrump.*

Gran looks at me and presses a finger to her lips as we move closer.

*Vrump. Vrump.*

Standing in the chamber are four of the strangest looking men. At least, they sort of look like men.

"Who are they, Gran?" I whisper, but she doesn't reply.

I tilt to look back around the hollow, into *our* chamber. They're not here, just there. *What on earth?* They cross the chamber, as if gliding on the wind, to take their places at their thrones.

"That man there," Gran begins eventually, gesturing, "well, a man of sorts – if humans could describe him – that is the formidable Lord North and I don't necessarily mean formidable in a positive sense, shall we say."

The man Gran is nodding towards, from here at least, is ridiculously tall. Draped from his broad, angular shoulders are floor-length thick velvety blue robes. Stitched across his chest, in a silver thread, almost as thick as rope, is an enormous letter N. I catch a glimpse of the others before they sit. Each 'Lord' as Gran calls them, has individual metallic-looking clasps holding their robes together. Not at the front, but down their backs. Lord North doesn't sit when the others do, but, instead, paces to and fro around the back of his throne. The candlelight catches the bright blue streak which runs down his slicked mane-like hair.

"Can they see us?" I whisper.

"No, but the Lords may ... sense us."

"How?"

"Because they are part of the Earth and because you are here."

"What does that mean?"

"You, my dear, are an important link between the past and the future; between our world and," nodding at the Lords, "theirs."

*What?*

I replay Gran's words, becoming aware that my breathing is rapid and shallow. *Our world and theirs? Dream. This must be a dream.*

Gran immediately detects my distress. One hand clutches under my elbow, steadying me. The other, she holds just inches from my chest. She doesn't speak, but I begin to feel the anxiety trickle away. I feel exhausted as I swim through so many waves of emotions, fearing now that I will drown in them. I want to cry out against the tidal surge, but Gran keeps her hand across my chest a moment longer, before pressing her forefinger to her lips once more.

"I declare this emergency meetin' of tha' High Council of Earth in session. This occurrence is unprecedented," begins Lord North, his voice as broad as his shoulders. "Tha' balance of our world and theirs and everythin'in existence since the Dawning has been disturbed. It must be restored by whatever means are necessary." He sounds Yorkshire born like me, but a more southern twang.

"Gran, I've never heard of the High Council of Earth. What is it?"

"Answers are coming, my dearest. For now, just listen."

From the E stitched onto his robe, I assume the one sat furthest from view is Lord East. He raises himself from his throne to address the council. He looks the most unlike Lord North, with the exception of height. I feel calmer. Gran doesn't stop me as I shuffle closer to the hollow. Lord East is a thin man with high set cheekbones, a long crooked nose and ears too large for his face. The robes he wears, like Lord North's, are thick and velvety too, but in rich Autumnal colours. Swathes of russets, light and dark golds and browns bleed together and compliment his cocoa skin. Lord North nods to acknowledge him. I can now see more of Lord North, too. His complexion is paper pale, kissed with blues and greens; his features not as fine as Lord East's. Ocean blue fills his eyes, and for a moment, I can actually see waves curling and crashing in them. I look at Gran, as if to check what I am seeing is real. She smiles, then winks.

"Haff any of you seen or spoken to our Almighty Mother?" enquires Lord East, stroking his wispy greying beard. His sharp tone rattles around the chamber.

"Her Lady Galtonia informed me, prior to our meeting, that she is in the grip of a fever and can't speak wi' anyone," replies Lord North turning his face away for a moment.

"So, my Lords, what proposals haff you?" asks Lord East.

"That is why we are 'ere. I can only speak for myself and those I represent. In truth, I am … unsure. Indeed, as I suspect, we all are," admits Lord North, who seems to be struggling with his own choice of words. "Wi'out speaking to Galtonia, we simply cannot know how to act. We must have some degree of patience."

"Patience?" Lord South stands, flicking his robes back and reaches for a red goblet. He takes the smallest of sips, then replaces it on the oak table. I catch a glimpse of a large golden S across his chest. He slams the palm of his claw-like hand onto the table. *Huh!* His sudden anger startles me.

"You ask us to have patience? You of all people! Ha! What happens if our Almighty Mother does not recover?"

*Who is this Almighty Mother they keep talking about?*

Lord South lowers his head for a brief moment. There is something creepy about his voice. It's thin and spindly.

"WHAT THEN?" he roars suddenly. "Without her, we, this High Council, do not exist!"

Startled, my hand finds Gran's.

"I don't agree," replies Lord North, jabbing his finger towards Lord South. "An' I am tellin' you, she will recover."

An already weary Lord East interrupts. "Can you be certain? No. Of course not. We're certain of nothing. Not now. Everything's changed. Perhaps irrecoverably." Lord East rubs his temples as if fighting off a headache.

*Maybe I should chuck a paracetamol through the hollow.* Lord knows I could do with one myself. Gran chuckles. Hmm, listening to my thoughts again.

"There has been an occurrence on an unprecedented level," begins Lord North looking at his fellow Lords, in turn. "That much we do know. But what evades us is detail, clarity. For we do not know what sort of occurrence we are dealing with. Summat in our world or theirs has acted as a catalyst that's for sure. Our whole universe is built on action and reaction. The sooner we speak with Galtonia again, the better. She must be able to discover something, anything that can begin a re-balancing." Lord North's cold stare is fixed. "You're rather quiet on this point, Lord West. Will you address your fellows, here and now, or sit brooding, as is always the case?"

I had been so mesmerised by the other Lords, I had barely noticed Lord West. He was the most difficult to see from our position. Leaning back on his throne, he kicks his legs up onto the table, much to the disgust and annoyance of the other Lords.

"Take your feet off the table, West," snarls Lord North, placing his balled fists onto it. Lord West waits, as entwining branches rise up from the chamber floor clasping a glass encrusted in silver and brimming with a red coloured juice. *That is so cool.* He knocks the drink back, tosses the glass, which disintegrates into the scattering of sand underneath the table. *How on earth can glass turn back to sand?* Again, I look back around the hollow. There is only carpet, here. But, where the Lords are, the floor is covered in leaves, soil and sand, which I hadn't noticed before. Eventually, Lord West takes his legs off the table. All of us await his response.

Gran raises my hand in hers and points. "Impressive, isn't it?" she whispers, meaning the chamber, I think.

"I love the inlay of gold on the floor," she continues. "Each of the four Lords sit at the pinnacle of the direction they reign over." I listen to Gran, but can't take my eyes off Lord West. He exchanges a stern look with each of his fellow councillors; as he turns to Lord South, I shudder at Lord West's scorched orange eyes. He looks so peculiar. Those eyes fill me with fear and I take a moment to drink in the rest of his features. Of all the Lords, it is Lord West who has the softest features, which compared to his eyes, doesn't look quite right. He is tall too, comparing his height against the rest, with narrow shoulders upon which sit layers of long, sleek straw-coloured hair. Like the others, his extravagant robes compliment his peach-coloured skin tones.

*How can this be real?*

"The first course of action, I believe, is to inform the tribes. All of them," begins Lord West, his tone regal. "By now, every living creature in Gaian will have experienced the turmoil our world is in. And in light of this, we cannot and should not keep them in the dark. For if we do, representatives of every tribe, every being and creature, dark and light, will beat down our door and demand answers ..." he pauses, sighs, then almost whispering to himself, says, "answers, my Lords, that we have not yet ascertained."

"Lord West appears the most affected," Gran says. "I can see it in his eyes."

"We must approach Galtonia again to try and rouse her. I will call upon the Wiccans; we need advice from their healers. I believe Althea is the leader of their clan," adds Lord West.

"It's a start," admits Lord North. "We shall summon Gal–"

But before Lord North can finish his sentence, a woman bursts through the chamber doors and glides across the floor towards the startled Lords. She is, without doubt, the most beautiful woman I've ever seen. Her golden robes flutter in slow motion like a bird being filmed. Her strawberry-red hair cascades around her shoulders, floating gently to and fro. Each candle flickers and crackles as the wind she has brought whistles around the chamber.

*Incredible!*

"Galtonia!" cries Lord North.

"I humbly beg your pardon my Lords, but I come with a message."

"You may speak freely inside these walls, Galtonia," announces Lord North.

"Our Almighty Mother has spoken to me," she begins, before pausing to catch her breath then bowing before each of the Lords. "She believes the fault lies, not in our world, but theirs."

"As I suspected," begins Lord South, but Lord North raises his hand for quiet.

"She needs the Elementals. The three of them must be brought to her," Galtonia continues.

*Three of them?*

"And, the Potential is her greatest defensive weapon. It must be moved to a place of safety and prepared."

*Weapon? Prepared? Potential?*

A shudder rockets up my spine like I've been hit at high voltage. Questions burst like fireworks, some bigger and brighter than others. Too many to know which to ask first.

# CHAPTER FIFTEEN

## 30th October 1821: Evelyn
### Hollow's Home

Unease has been my constant companion. Something is different. Something about this day has shifted. It is a feeling that has shackled itself to me. Clasping my hand gently around a piece of lavender I squeeze a bud, releasing a droplet of its exquisite aroma, the calming effect of which is instant and appreciated.
I trail my hand through the abundance of stems.

I feel utterly torn and plagued by one single question: *Do I continue to allow my children their freedom?*

If I suddenly keep them bound inside these walls, they will suspect something is amiss, especially Constance, who is approaching that delicate age. It feels unnatural to me to restrict their freedom in their own home.

I continue to roam the grounds of our estate. Windsor House has survived centuries of wars and kept every generation of Walsinghams safe. It always will; of that I am sure. Adoring the winter jasmine, all the while I keep Harriet in view. The mahonia has begun in earnest to change. Its bright yellow leaves now dappled with the purples and reds it will soon display through winter.

Anxiety has befriended me once more in the time it has taken me to reach the lowest point of the grounds, despite the lavender. I can see clearly into the meadow. At the farthest point, Harriet stands, hands on her hips, staring at the Hollow Tree. I am overwhelmed with a desire to rush to her side and distance her from it, but I regain my composure in the time it takes me to cross the meadow, weaving through dozens and dozens of newly planted alders and elms.

Upon hearing me through the rustle of long grasses, Harriet tenses and examines her petticoats.

"Harriet, please tell me that's not another one ruined?" I ask as I finally reach her.

"Mother, did you hear that Captain Pennington's eldest son built a raft twice the size of mine just last week, but nearly died when he tested it on the stream? Wouldn't that have been ghastly? I would be terribly upset for the Captain and Mrs Pennington. And what a waste! All George's hard work would have been for nothing as it would certainly have ended up drifting all the way to the ocean."

*Clever fox.*

Harriet does her usual avoidance trick. A future politician perhaps, now we women have been bestowed with the right to vote.

"Harriet, I asked you a question."

She turns towards me, clears her throat and adopts an expression that pleads both ignorance and innocence.

"Well, I did tell you I was going to be busy today, Mother. I can't be outdone by a boy now, can I? When is Father going to be home?"

I observe this mud-ridden, dishevelled daughter of mine.

"Do you know, Harriet, I could have sworn that you were a girl when you were born. That's why your father and I named you Harriet and not Henry."

A scowl sweeps over her face, which amuses me greatly.

"I will never be as perfect as Constance. But, I am very certain that my being so like Papa as I am is most tolerable, perhaps even agreeable."

Harriet's defence is a clever one. She knows I can find little to fault in that argument. Harriet is *exactly* like my husband, William. Always busy, always thinking, always seeking out new things and adventures. But then she reminds me so much of myself, too, at her age.

"Your father will be home very soon, young lady, and he will not, no matter how fine a creation you have endeavoured to build, be happy to see you looking like that at the dinner table. Now, go and find Mary, quickly and dress for dinner."

"Thank you, Mother," she yells, her speed fighting against the long grasses, before she reaches the gardens.

"And pray to Almighty God, young lady, that Mary isn't minded to scold you for ruining yet another petticoat!"

As I watch her disappear beyond the hedgerows, a shiver skates down my spine. But I will not let fear and anxiety overwhelm me. I refuse to let it. *How to protect her. All three of them. This requires further thought.*

I march over to the Hollow Tree, emboldened. A spell whilst we sleep gives me more time to prepare. Anxiety challenges anger from deep within my gut, but it is anger that triumphs. Pressing my hand firmly to my chest, steadying myself, I crouch down immediately in front of the Hollow Tree. I lose myself in its shadows for a brief moment.

"You cannot have her! I know you're listening, so hear me. You cannot have her. You cannot have *any* of my children."

# CHAPTER SIXTEEN

# 30th October 2021: Hannah
## Confrontation

"Hannah, dear, it's time to wake," Joyce says as if she's waking a baby from its slumber. I squint and try to make out my surroundings. "She's coming round now."

*Must be talking to Gran.*

I forgot!

*Joyce knows everything.*

I pull myself up, eager to see her.

"There now," Joyce says stroking the tangled hair from my face. "Welcome back, young lady. We really must run a comb through this."

"Aren't you meant to be guarding my mother?"

Joyce smiles, then winks. "You mean 'protecting', I think. So, we know something, don't we?"

I can't help but giggle at her use of the royal 'we'.

"Yes, *we* do."

"Your mother is in a side room just there," she nods then flicks up her nurse's watch. "And, as of four minutes ago, was still sleeping. I will return to her in a moment or two."

"Now, my darling girl," begins Gran from her chair behind Joyce, very much alive. "Down to business, as they say. I have more to tell you before your mother wakes. You see, Hannah, something has happened and it affects you. You may have detected that from Galtonia's message."

Gran shuffles forward pulling the chair with her before taking a long, deep breath as if its she's about to scale Snowden.

"No need for machines and wires anymore then, Gran?" My eyebrow raises.

"Ghastly things."

"But often necessary," chimes Joyce.

I glance around the room trying to get my bearings. It's like a hospital ward, only much, much larger, with high windows and even higher ceilings. There are two rows of beds on either side of central pillars, which run the length of the room. Surprisingly, we are the only ones in there, but I guess the residents mostly stay in their own rooms.

"I cannot say with any certainty exactly what has happened, but you have a vital role to play in events."

"Not bloody likely!" None of us even heard the door. Before I can say a word, Mum is at my side, flinging her arms around me crying, which always makes me cry.

"I'm okay, Mum. Really I am."

"Oh Han, you scared me half to death," she sobs. Taking my head in her hands for the second time today, she examines my face.

"Almost," Gran adds.

Anger ignites in Mum's eyes like Gran's just dowsed her

in lighter fuel.

Mum turns. "Don't you dare talk to her! Or me for that matter. How can you have the audacity? You have no right …"

Mum's flicked that switch of hers and it's flashing at an alarming rate.

"I have every right, Caroline. *You* saw to that."

"MUM, STOP IT! Please?" I say, soaking up the determined tears with my sleeve.

"Everything will be alright my darling," Gran smiles at me.

"DON'T YOU DARE TALK TO HER! THIS IS ALL YOUR FAULT."

"I think you know that's not entirely true, Caroline!"

*What does Gran mean by that?*

Her reply stuns Mum into silence. No one speaks. Then, just as Joyce begins to open her mouth, Mum jabs her finger towards her chest. "And you! Did *she* tell you to poison me?" she says flinging her arm out, directing her accusation (I think it's called) at Gran.

"Was my mother the one instructing you, like a good little nursemaid, to administer her sleeping potions?"

"What?" I ask.

"Oh yes, Han. The master and the puppeteer playing their little games," Mum replies.

"You know very well that I am the alchemist, Caroline, not your mother."

Mum glares at Joyce, then Gran. I've never, ever seen my mum look this cross. In fact, infuriated would be a better word.

"Caroline, may I speak?" Gran asks quietly.

"I do not want to hear what you have to say. Come on Hannah, we're going."

"But you wanted to speak to her," I begin. "You *needed* to speak to her about the accident."

Mum looks betrayed. *I don't understand – have I said something wrong?*

"Joyce assured me you were okay. It was nothing, you told her, Caroline."

Silence.

"Was it nothing?" Gran asks.

"We didn't hit a tree. Or swerve to miss a fox. Something hit us," Mum explains.

"Something?" enquires Joyce.

"You don't know?" asks Gran. I'm desperate to interrupt and blurt it all out, but I know I should leave it to Mum.

"No. We didn't see anything. Except after, a pack of silver foxes appeared right in front of us. They're endangered. So, seeing a whole pack really was quite extraordinary. And … Hannah saw something on the car. We *both* saw something on the car."

"Silver foxes are rare," says Gran casting a look at Joyce. "What did you see, Hannah?" Gran continues uncrossing her legs to reposition herself.

I glance at Mum, who nods. "A claw mark all the way down the side of the car. But it was, like, giant-sized."

Immediately, Joyce tenses and moves to my side. Gran stands, her eyes flick from window to door as though whatever made the claw mark is about to come bursting through the door.

# CHAPTER SEVENTEEN

## Lightning Bolt

I don't know how long we stand there 'on pins' as Mum would say, but it feels like forever. Eventually, Gran and Joyce drop their guard a little after exchanging 'the look' which means they've 'spoken'. *I so want to know.*

"I'm more concerned by the appearance of silver foxes," begins Gran. "Someone beyond these walls knows more than we do."

"If it wasn't you or me, then who? Galtonia?" suggests Joyce.

"No, they're the last thing she'd send and certainly not gargoyles, if indeed they were."

*What on earth are they talking about?*

"Look, I don't know what on earth is going on here, but I don't like it," barks Mum. "And I want nothing to do with this. We're leaving because clearly, there is *nothing* wrong with you."

"But there is something wrong with me," I say.

Mum sneers at Gran. "What have you filled her head with?"

I find myself inching in front of Gran, suddenly afraid of what Mum might do. It dawns on me then that Gran isn't using her empath power to calm Mum down. At least, it certainly doesn't seem like she is.

"We're not leaving, Mum. Not until you listen to what Gran has to say."

She stops pacing the room and another look of betrayal etches across her face. This time I *do* understand why. But Mum knows I am as stubborn as she is, if not worse. Other than literally dragging me back to York … Mum knows I won't budge. Eventually, she huffs and turns to stare out at the dark blue hues of the sky. I don't feel like I've betrayed her; at the very least Gran deserves the chance to explain.

*"That was very brave of you Hannah, defending your grandmother like that."*

"So you can read my mind too?" I stare at Joyce, open-mouthed.

*"Hear your thoughts, yes. Talk to you, yes."*

*So Joyce can hear my thoughts just as easily as Gran can.*

*"Actually, my hearing is a little better than your Grandmother's."*

*"Joyce, do you mind getting out of my head?"*

Sorry, she mouths. Joyce blinks, but it lasts a second or two, like she's disconnecting the Wi-Fi or something.

*I really need my own password protection!*

Gran is now concentrating on Mum's face; perhaps reading her thoughts this time. *I wonder if Mum knows.* They both seem lost.

All too quickly the sky darkens. From behind the blackest

of clouds a streak of light twists down piercing the glass. The blade of light is so thin. I have never seen lightning like it. It spirals around the room, like a missile searching for its target. Half a second later it strikes Joyce in the chest, flinging her to the floor, knocking her out cold. Her body slides a few feet down the ward.

"Joyce!" I crash down onto my knees skidding to her side. "Gran, do something."

"I can't. It's a lightning bolt."

"What sort of lightning bolt was that?" snaps Mum, horrified.

"Not the sort you have ever seen before," replies Gran.

"What the hell does that mean?" she snaps again.

"For crying out loud, Caroline, you know I hate the H-word."

Mum ignores her and kneels at my side, placing her hands on my shoulders.

"Gran, if you won't soddin' well do anything, then at least tell us what's happening?"

*I can't believe Gran is just standing there!*

"All these profanities, girls! So unladylike," she huffs, resting against the iron bedstead.

I glare at Gran. Her best friend gets struck by lightning and all she's worried about is our use of a few choice words. It's not like I'd actually use something really bad.

"Gran?"

"Very well, very well."

*I can't believe Gran is so calm about this.*

"The lightning bolt contains a message from someone. I don't know who at this point. Due to bolts being a pure form of light, they are almost impossible to break or corrupt should someone want to intercept a message."

"So, someone has just sent us a message that no one but us, or at least Joyce, must find out about?" I ask, feeling fear awaken in the pit of my stomach.

"Precisely."

Joyce jerks up gasping for air.

"You're okay, Joyce. You're okay," I say squeezing her hand.

"But you're not. Hold hands, now!" Joyce orders as me and Mum pull her up.

"What's happening?" asks Mum.

"We must form a circle of light," begins Gran, standing up, clearly shaken. "Quickly!"

"You know what the message is, don't you?" I accuse Gran.

"Yes, Hannah. Now I do."

"But, how? You said nothing could get in, break it?" *Gran must have tapped into Joyce's head as soon as she woke up.*

"Every one of us must hold hands," Joyce screeches. "Now!"

Mum has no choice. Joyce yanks her hand, Gran grabs mine and we form a squarish-sort-of-circle.

Gran begins. "Come forth into the light. Protected be upon first sight," and then raises her face upwards towards the ceiling, expectantly. A wave of nausea washes over me.

"Come forth into the light. Protected be upon first sight," follows Joyce. "Now you, Caroline."

"No. Not until you tell me why."

"Come forth into the light. Protected be upon first sight," I say, feeling goose bumps rise across my skin. Shock falls down Mum's face.

"Mum, just say it!"

"Come forth into the light. Protected be upon first sight," she mumbles, but it's enough.

The chorus continues over and over until I lose count.

"Let the light in."

"Let the light in."

"Let the light in."

# CHAPTER EIGHTEEN

## Galtonia's Warning

A tiny light appears in the middle of our circle, just like the one that revealed Gran. It looks like one of those fire flower things, only brighter. The hair on my arms stands on end like a million little lightning conductors. I realise we are all suspended in the air, holding on, but only to each other. Cool.

"Come forth into the light. Protected be upon first sight," Joyce repeats one final time, her voice clear, loud. Mum, brow furrowed, concentrates on the tiny light. *Has she even realised we're in the air?*

Deep within the heart of the light, the shape of a woman begins to form. Translucent at first, but as the light fades the more real she becomes. Not just a vision any more. I know her! Galtonia looks exactly the same, but perhaps even more beautiful than I remember. I swallow the sudden urge to reach out and touch that strawberry-coloured hair of hers, which glimmers under the fluorescent lights. Galtonia's eyes are like pools of gold catching the sheen of her creamy skin. She looks at each one of us around the circle. I glance at Mum; her mouth now wide open. I can't help but snigger. Galtonia nods to my mum and in a sort of trance-like state, Mum nods back.

As the final dot of light vanishes our feet eventually find the ground.

"Bloody hell!" gasps Mum stumbling as we land.

*That would be a no, then.*

"Hannah." Galtonia steps forward taking my hands, her touch warm, her voice soft. "It is such a pleasure, no, an honour to finally meet you. What a beautiful young woman you have grown into."

*Beautiful? Me?*

"The … er … honour is … all mine."

"Oh, you are sweet." Unexpectedly, she bows to me. I decide it would be rude not to bow back.

*"No!"* Joyce's voice booms into my head. *"She will be insulted if you bow back to her. You are ranked a little higher than her, so to speak."*

*"Ranked? We're not in the army, Joyce."*

*"Just leave it,"* interrupts Gran with a glare, albeit a very small one. *I'm 'ranked' higher than Galtonia? That's ridiculous, ranking people.*

"I will have to curtail the formal greetings, as I come on a matter of great urgency, Eleanor."

Mum still looks shell-shocked. "You okay?" I whisper.

Mum, brow furrowed, looks like she's about to start a tirade of abuse of which Gran will almost certainly bear the brunt, but then comes the lavender.

*"Thanks, Gran. I think Mum really needs it."*

A second or two later, Mum shakes herself from the haze and raises her eyebrow in my direction. "She *bowed* to you?"

I shrug, desperately wanting to laugh, but Joyce 'ahems' in our direction.

"The news I have, unfortunately, is not to be borne lightly for it is Gaia herself who has ordered me to you."

Who?

Both Gran and Joyce's mouths hit the floor, before they instinctively reach for one another.

"You are both now aware of the situation and I believe Hannah has witnessed some of what is happening, although I understand you have not yet *fully* appraised her of the grave situation we now find ourselves in."

*What grave situation?*

"That is correct," says Gran.

Like an army cadet attached to its squadron, questions begin marching, forming a long line that trails right the way to the back of my mind.

*Here we go again!*

More questions.

More answers.

More truths.

More lies?

My heart sinks, a wreck on an ocean floor.

"I bring you a direct command, Eleanor."

"A command?" Gran asks.

"Yes. It is this: that you take Hannah, without delay, to the Hollow Tree."

"Goodness!" cries Joyce.

"WHAT?" bellows Mum.

I thought the lavender would last longer than that!

"It is perfectly safe, Caroline. I swear on my life," replies Galtonia.

"It's not your life I'm worried about!"

"Mum!"

*Uh, embarrassing.*

"Why has …?" Gran begins, but Galtonia continues.

"As of this moment, Caroline, you have no choice. Gaia believes there may be more to the situation and has felt for some time that there is someone whom cannot …" Galtonia appears pained by her own words, "… be trusted and she suspects betrayal at the highest level. And that the traitor lies within the High Council."

"Surely not?" Joyce now looks completely overwhelmed and perches on the edge of a bed. Not surprising, considering the force of the lightning bolt that hit her, too. I squeeze her hand as Galtonia's warning sinks in. *I wonder if I can read Joyce's mind.*

"Calm yourself," says Gran. "So Gaia believes, genuinely

believes, one of the Lords is plotting against her?"

*Who are they talking about? Who is this 'Gaia'?*

"Unequivocally."

I picture the four Lords sat on their grand thrones and wonder which of them the traitor is.

"I understand why you question this, Eleanor," Galtonia continues. "Difficult as that may be to accept, but yes, that is what she believes."

"But that would be high treason."

"What possible reason could there be?" interrupts Joyce.

"To usurp her. That is why she sent me with this message. The council know nothing of our meeting here today. I am the only one she has spoken her fears to."

Mum walks over to the bed as if her legs are about to give way and perches on the edge, but leaves some distance between herself and Joyce.

"She is wise to be cautious," nods Gran pouring them both a glass of water.

"She believes Hannah may be her most powerful ally, but equal to that, the most high profile target. She has despatched Althea, Elric and Lilith to bring the elementals to her immediately."

"The elementals, as well?"

"Yes. The gravity of the situation, you now can comprehend, Joyce. And, furthermore, because she knows

114

Evelyn will not let her children go without a fight, she feels it only prudent to have, well, a contingency plan."

Galtonia bows her head in my direction ever so slightly and it feels like fear has put its arm around my shoulders. I shake it off, not wanting to give in to it.

"I won't be anyone's damn contingency plan!"

"Over my dead body!" Mum snarls, rising up and practically squaring up to Galtonia.

Gran ignores my protest, but she can't ignore Mum's. Or, rather, Mum won't let herself be ignored.

"You're not taking Hannah anywhere without my permission."

"Caroline, you can either be part of this or not. I assume your only desire is your daughter's safety?" Gran doesn't wait for a reply. "Or, my alchemist friend will work her magic once more. Your choice."

Mum, defeated, sits back down holding her head in her hands. *I know exactly how she feels*. I move to sit between her and Joyce. I don't know who's taken the news worse. Questions continue marching in their thousands.

One-two. One-two. One-two.

I take Mum's hand because I don't know what else I can do. She looks up, strokes my hair. Her eyes reflect one thing – guilt.

*Why guilt?*

"But why Evelyn's children? And why then?" asks Gran. "Some event of significance happened around that time, and it was Evelyn's children who were the elemental heirs back then. It would have been before Victoria took the throne."

"So, two periods of significance, one now and one prior to, what, 1830? Two events, two catalysts perhaps. But set in motion … how? And all by the hand of the would-be usurper," adds Gran.

"Yes, we believe so. That is what she believes the visions show, but sometimes, Eleanor, delirium sets in when the fever is at its worst."

Overcome, Galtonia turns away, perhaps composing herself. Tuning in to their conversation I can't actually believe what I'm hearing.

One-two. One-two. One-two.

# CHAPTER NINETEEN

# 30th October 1821: Evelyn
## Pentagram

I stare into the flames, feeling their warmth on my face, only faintly aware of William pacing the room. I have never held a fear for my marriage; William knows what I am and accepted me from the very start of our courtship. To this day, he has never once faltered in his loyalty. But that loyalty will now, for the first time it seems, be put to the test. I share his distress, but shall not wallow in it.

"Are you certain, Evelyn? Truly certain?"

"Yes."

"Beyond all reasonable doubt?"

"You and your reasonable doubt. Yes, my love, I am."

"Then what must we do?"

"Light the lanterns. I will begin in here."

Quietly, not to awaken the children or Mary, William leaves the room taking the larger of the lamps. Opening the cabinet door, I remove a panel from within the side wall behind which sit five pillar candles. Collecting them, I move to the centre of the room. Concentrating my energy, I twirl my finger in a tiny circular motion and watch the carpet roll up neatly revealing the pentagram. A favourite of mine amongst many hidden throughout the house – the green and gold filigree catches in the candlelight – as I continue lighting all but one of the candles.

I move to the window and wait for William to come into view. I scan the darkness of night for any movement whilst waiting for William. Making haste, I see his lantern swing to and fro, lighting his way as he crosses the grounds towards the final point of the external marker. Each marker sits in the guise of a Corinthian column, identifiable by our family name – Walsingham – engraved into the frieze. Together, the columns form a pentagram that encompasses our home. Now, I can just make out William's face against the flickering of the flame. Suddenly, confirming my suspicions, a streak of light darts through the trees to the east.

Something *is* out there!

I throw open the window. "William! Hurry!" My voice whistles across the gardens.

"What is it?"

"There!" I point. William, enveloped by darkness, scans the grounds, but whatever it was has disappeared.

*Not for long, I fear.*

He lights the final lantern which lies just beyond the Hollow Tree. He leaves the final column and begins his way back. Part way across the gardens, a ruby-coloured light spirals through the trees again.

"Run, William!"

It takes him only minutes to arrive back at the courtyard steps. I throw myself into the centre of the pentagram and light the final candle.

*"I am the Light Keeper. Hear my call.*
*Those who trespass, will wither and fall.*
*I give you blood, passed into light,*
*Protect the Sacred through this night."*

My hair falls as I pull the pin out. I draw it across my finger letting a single droplet of blood fall into each flame. I repeat the spell for each candle. Each drop of blood seeks out the next point, compelled by its desire to bond and complete the pentagram that surrounds me.

*"I cast a pentagram out this night*
*To protect our home beyond dawn's first light.*
*I am the Light Keeper. Hear my call.*
*Those who trespass, will wither and fall.*
*With Sacred blood, passed into light,*
*Send this pentagram out of sight."*

William returns to see ribbons of red fire burst forth from each candle. They each spiral out seeking their external posts. The force knocks William to the ground. My fingers reach out touching his. He nods reassuringly. At each pinnacle the ribbon of fire crackles, entwines, leaving only embers to fade into the night air.

"Is it done?" he asks.

"It is done."

He breathes a sigh of relief.

"It is done," I repeat.

No creature of darkness can break a Light Keeper's spell.

My spell.

# CHAPTER TWENTY

## 30th October 2021: Hannah
### Lightning Can Strike Twice

Galtonia and Joyce throw themselves between me and the window. One of them shoves me to the ground, hard.

*Boom!*

Before Mum can ask what is happening, or I can pull myself up, flashes of lightning crack and fill the room. *It's outside.* What's all the panic for?

"It's a thunderstorm, Gran."

*Crack!*

*Crack!*

I flinch. Like I said, I hate storms. Surely, this is overkill though? The lightning's close, but thankfully it's not flying around the room, ready to take one of us down. I push myself up a little.

"Stay down, Hannah!" Joyce shouts. She pulls an orb, which glows blue, from her pocket. *Cool.* Gran, being closest to the window, skirts across the bed and pulls Mum down. *Gran's fast!*

"It's just a storm," says Mum, but now a Titanic-sized sinking feeling churns in my gut.

"Caroline, stay down here. For once, do as you are told. Remember, I'm still *your* mother!"

Gran then turns to Joyce. "Something isn't right," she

murmurs. "Can you feel it?"

"Yes. Energy shift."

A third bolt strikes causing something to burst into flames outside, the force blows out the windows. Shielding my face, I wait for the glass to rain down on us, but it doesn't. I see Gran turn every deadly shard into a sand cloud. *Could have done with that earlier* I think, touching the cuts on my cheek. Beneath us the earth rumbles. Doors and cabinets around the ward begin to shudder, some unlatch and swing. Glass panes crack, fall and shatter. I try to push myself up further to see even more, but Galtonia growls a warning, then unclasps her robe, then throws it over me. It never once touches my body, but hovers like an ocean wave lapping inches above my head. I shuffle to one side to get out from under it, but it moves when I do. I shuffle forwards – seeing the bottom of the doorway – but, again, it tracks my movements.

"What's happening?" Mum yells, pushing a tea trolley out of the way, as she attempts to crawl across to me. Walls shudder, plaster cracks and chunks begin to fall to the ground. Mum freezes, shielding her head, unsure of which way to go. I try again to crawl out from under the cloak but this time it lowers and forces me down.

*Argh!*

The room shakes violently.

I drop onto my side, pressing my face into my knees and concentrate on breathing.

Mum shouts again, "What's happening?"

I can't see her.

"Get under the cloak, Caroline. Now!" orders Gran.

All of the sudden, the cloak billows up and Joyce shoves Mum under it, then vanishes again. I pull Mum into me and we clutch each other as she curls around me. The cloak settles leaving no more than a few inches above our heads. *It clearly has the ability to protect us, somehow.* I desperately want to see, but the more I attempt to move, the more the cloak lowers itself. Forced onto our backs, we press our hands against it. With pleading eyes, I beg Mum to do something. *We probably can't stop it, no matter how much we want to.*

"I don't know what to do, Han," cries Mum.

*I CAN'T BREATHE!*

My palms slam against the floor.

The cloak rises a few inches.

*Gran heard!*

"Galtonia! Ready yourself!" shouts Gran. The trembling earth continues. Cracks begin to appear in the tiled floor beneath us. Lights flicker. In the distance, I can hear residents' cries and the clatter of trollies and wheelchairs between the rumbles.

*They must be so scared.*

"Prepare for what?" I yell from underneath the robe. I push against the smoothness of the cloak, which doesn't budge.

"Let me up!"

My knuckles drain of colour. I desperately want, no, need to see.

*What's happening?*

"Gran, I can't breathe under this! Please! It's still too low."

Almost instantly, the cloak raises a few inches higher, giving me and Mum space to move and breathe. Together, we roll onto our stomachs.

Is this what an earthquake feels like?

*Shouldn't we all be stood in a doorway or something?*

But then a feeling creeps over me that this is no normal storm, or earthquake, even. I've never heard of earthquakes in Norfolk? Not knowing what is happening only makes my heart heave faster.

*Grrawrrrrgh!*

"Huh!"

I throw my hands over my ears as the noise ricochets around the room like a stray bullet. My imagination flits from one possible cause to another; each seemingly more and more insane.

"Do something!" shouts Mum, edging to see what is going

on.

*"What's happening, Gran? Please!"*

She doesn't reply.

Concentrate!

I know I have the ability to make them hear me, and maybe I can hear them.

*"Joyce?"*

There's no point in shouting, so I focus harder, picturing them in the room somewhere.

*"Please? What's happening?"*

Still no reply, but I open my eyes to see Galtonia's cloak shaking, its patterns ripple and fade just enough, leaving an almost transparent force field floating over me and Mum.

*Grrawrrrrgh!*

"What is that?"

Screams rush up my throat, scorching it; chest vibrating, ears ringing. My hands cup my ears again. My screams pale in comparison to Mum's. She pulls me over her body and I press myself into her back, peering across her shoulder. I can't take my eyes off it! Nearby Gran crouches behind an upturned bed, bellowing something at Galtonia and Joyce, but I can't see them at all.

Only ... it.

The mange-covered creature swings in through an enormous cavity in the roof and hangs gorilla-like from a thick beam that remains intact. Its nostrils flare as it sniffs the air like a wild dog seeking its prey. Its enormity casts a deep shadow into the room. Snarls slice through the air like a samurai sword from its hound-like face. Crescent-shaped spikes line the length of its arms and back catching the moonlight as dusk settles in. It snorts again, its vast chest expands, rumbling as it rises. Part of me can't bear to look at it, but neither can part of me look away from its ferocious amber eyes as they scan the hospital ward.

*What is it looking for?*

It stops. It sniffs sharply in all directions; amber eyes narrowing, marking its target: Mum!

Her trembling body infects mine. I grasp her tightly. Sparks fly into the air, crackling and bursting around its head, temporarily blinding it. That *must* be Gran.

Galtonia sweeps to our side peering under the cloak.

"Hannah, have you cut yourself?"

"No. No!"

"Caroline?"

"I don't think so." Galtonia reaches in and brushes Mum's hair from her face and there, trickling down from her right brow is a thin line of blood.

"Dammit!" cries Galtonia, glaring at Mum. "Stay down."

The cloak lowers, leaving little room, but it isn't the cloak that is making me breathless now. Mum keeps her eyes fixed firmly on the creature. I search the room for Gran who is now at Joyce's side. Blocked by the rows of beds, and from this position, I can only see their feet shuffling, then darting forwards and backwards, like a dance. From their direction, bright blue globes fly up to strike the beast, but it bats them away, each time its grunts puncture the air.

"Why won't it die?" Mum shouts panic-stricken.

Joyce – now on all fours – ducks and slides under bed after bed, moving closer to us. She's unhurt, as far as I can tell.

*"They are powerful beasts."*

Mum probably hasn't even realised Joyce answered her without speaking. *"It wants your blood, Caroline. It thinks you are the Potential. It can smell your blood and nothing will stop it ..."*

Nothing will stop it.

Nothing.

*But why Mum?*

Gran retreats back towards us, too. I hadn't realised how far down the ward they were. Far too close to the beast, which still hangs from part of the demolished roof. The whole building groans as debris from the walls and the ceiling continues to fall. I flinch at each chunk of plaster and stone that strikes the cloak, but it just flexes, barely registering the impact.

Across the room, Galtonia moulds orbs of fire, like a potter. She lines them up one by one, suspended in the air, ready to fire at the beast. Now side-by-side, Joyce and Gran combine their violet-coloured orbs, unleashing shot after shot. The creature snarls and whines in pain, but its response is to rip an enormous chunk of the wall away from the ruins and launch it towards its attackers. Gran throws her arms in the air again, but her strength is fading. Joyce grabs half a dozen of Galtonia's fire-filled orbs launching them as it readjusts its position to hide in the shadows as the lights crackle, flicker and die. Moonlight spreads throughout the ward.

*Bhump.*

*Bhump.*

*Bhump.*

Walls rupture. Chunks of stone crack apart.

"Joyce!" cries Gran shoving her out of the way as a huge chunk of plaster plummets to the ground. It misses Joyce but Gran can't move fast enough so throws her arms up over her head as a huge deluge of rubble buries her.

No!

"Mum!"

"Gran!"

*"Gran, answer me! Gran!"*

But she doesn't.

Mum pulls herself up, as Joyce slides across the floor and scrambles under Galtonia's cloak, forcing Mum to retreat.

"No! We have to go." Joyce barks.

"But, Gran?" I snap.

"She's alive. I can feel her heartbeat. But we must get you out of here."

"We're not leaving her!" cries Mum.

*We can't.*

"If we don't leave now, we all die!" cries Galtonia raising the cloak up higher and yanking me up. Joyce holds her hand out.

"Your choice, Caroline. Your mother or your daughter."

Mum takes it without hesitation. I burst into tears, as we dart through a door, which hangs on its last hinge. I beg Galtonia to help Gran. *We can't leave her!* With her cloak still suspended, Galtonia pushes her hands through the air and like a falling feather, the cloak glimmers against the moon, then shrouds the rubble under which Gran lies hurt and alone.

"The cloak will protect her."

*But for how long?*

# CHAPTER TWENTY-ONE

## Bait

The four of us hurtle down the corridor as walls crumble.

"What is that thing?" yells Mum breathlessly.

"A typhon. They are blood beasts," replies Galtonia.

"You mean like vampires?" I ask.

"Yes, insofar as they thirst for blood," says Joyce.

"Are vampires real?"

*Please say no. Please say no.*

"No, of course they aren't," replies Joyce – like vampires being real is ridiculous and a creature the size of an elephant, that moves like a gorilla, with the strength of an ox that thirsts for blood, isn't!

Pausing at a set of exit doors, we catch our breath. That's when I notice Galtonia and Joyce exchange a look. Plotting again.

*I hate not being able to hear.*

"I agree," replies Joyce. "Left, down the stairs at the end of the corridor."

"Wait! Agree to what?"

"I'll explain, but we've got to keep moving, Hannah," replies Joyce.

In the distance we can hear the typhon smashing through walls and shattering windows. Avoiding huge slabs of plaster and ceiling tiles swinging to and fro, I follow in

Mum's footsteps as we descend to the basement.

*What if the whole building collapses on us?*

Joyce pauses, then looks up to the fluorescent green sign: Fire Exit. Through its frosted glass panels, blue flashing lights catch our attention, as a wail of sirens draw closer and closer.

"We can't let the police see the creature, otherwise many more will die," warns Joyce.

"Then let's hook the fish," suggests Galtonia.

"Are you saying I'm bait?" asks Mum aghast.

"I am." There's coldness in Galtonia's reply that makes my entire body shudder. That, or the fact that a giant freak of a creature is trying to kill my mum.

Leaving the cries of residents, nurses and carers to fade behind us, Joyce, between breaths, explains that the typhon won't take long to pick up Caroline's scent and draw it away from the residents. I daren't think how many could die.

*What happens if Gran's one of them?*

Joyce holds up her hand. Stops. Then opens the door, checking each way. The corridors are filled with cold artificial lights, which click and flicker.

Galtonia rips a small piece from one of her skirts and wipes the blood from Mum's brow.

"Caroline, wipe it across the wall," she gestures.

Joyce approaches me and from the look on her face, I

realise she's 'spoken' with Galtonia again. My stomach flips.

"Hannah, give me your hand."

"Why?"

"Do you want to save your grandmother?"

"Of course I do! How can you ask me that?"

"Then hold out your hand." I do. Joyce turns it over, then takes a safety pin from her pocket and bends the clasp away.

I snatch my hand back. "What are you doing?"

"We need a diversion tactic. Trust me, Hannah. This will work," she explains, taking my hand and drawing the pin across my palm to leave a thin line of blood. It stings like mad, but it's a small sacrifice to save Gran.

"This should confuse the beast for a while. Now, run down as far as that last door on the left. Wipe your blood on its handle and once on the wall half way between. Hurry!"

With our blood daubed across the walls, Galtonia tears another piece of leaf-like fabric from her skirt and bandages my hand. After a few seconds, the leaf begins melting into it. I watch as the cut knits back together.

"Don't spill another drop."

*Incredible. Maybe she'll heal the scratches on my face.*

Galtonia turns to Mum and purses her lips, blowing an icy blast across her brow. "That should hold for a little while, but we may need a drop more." Mum winces.

Nausea stirs as we run back in the direction of the stairs, towards the creature, but as we reach a large grill on the wall, I understand why. Galtonia whirls her finger in tiny circles undoing every little screw before removing the grill.

*Grrawrrrrgh!*

Our bodies freeze.

Screams scrape down walls bleeding into our ears.

*This is all our fault.*

I clasp my mouth not wanting to throw up again. Leading the way, Joyce climbs up and crawls along the air vent and we follow staying as close as possible. Mum huffs, struggling for breath. Joyce then stops at a crossroads in the vent. She looks left, right and dead ahead.

"Right, Hannah. Time to spill." Joyce pulls a handkerchief from her trouser pocket. Queasiness runs through me as I pull at the thin line of knitted flesh. Blood seeps into the cloth. Why hasn't Joyce used Mum's?

Galtonia sniffs the air. "That's enough."

*Can Galtonia smell blood, too?*

She freezes my wound this time and the skin knits back together, leaving only a faint line.

"Crawl down the left vent. It leads back to the kitchens. Stuff the cloth into the grill. The fans will ensure the scent is circulated. I'll wait here for you. Joyce, take Caroline and get a head start."

I shuffle down the vent which is no larger than a water slide. How on earth did they expect the typhon to squeeze along the vents? Or would it just smash its way through? Sliding down the vent on my knees, I keep my wounded hand raised.

The typhon's wails draw closer. I imagine the police hearing the sound and realising it isn't an earthquake that's struck Attleborough. I freeze as the beast cries out again. It sounds strange, but it's like I can almost understand its cries.

*Frustration?*

Of course! Frustration at not being able to locate its target – Mum. Suddenly the vents clatter as walls shudder.

*Everyone must be so afraid.*

The noise alone will scare them half to death. We have to draw it away from the home, to save as many lives as possible.

Including Gran's.

I roll the blood-soaked cloth like a sausage roll and stuff it between the holes in the vents.

*Maybe I should …*

Pulling at the torn skin on my palm, I ball my fist. Ow! Blood seeps through my fingers and begins to drip. I wipe it all over the grill and finally on the cloth. It should be enough. My palm stings like mad as I cradle it. I blow cool breath over the wound, stupidly expecting it to freeze. I guess only Galtonia can do that. Pushing myself back down the vents, I see her, crouched into the small space.

"What took you so long?"

The sharpness in her tone stings almost as much as the palm of my hand.

"Go!" she orders.

Ahead, I can hear Mum and Joyce as cool crisp air tickles my cheeks. I drink it in. Mum pulls me through the grill, then Galtonia. Joyce replaces it then, conjuring a flame on the tip of her finger, seals the grill shut. *Seriously!*

Mum looks exhausted. "Are you okay?" she asks.

"Yeah. You?"

She nods, looking bewildered.

"Joyce, how do we get Gran?"

Just then the ground underneath begins shaking. I hold onto Mum. We stumble as the building shakes violently. It begins like an avalanche … walls crumble …

"Quick! To the gardens!" Joyce calls.

Legs move faster than thoughts.

"There!" calls Joyce redirecting us to the far side of the lawn where the conservatory, amazingly, still stands. Behind us, cries of help come from residents at broken windows.

"We have to help them!"

"We cannot. You'll get yourself killed," says Joyce.

"But you're both witches, or something. You have enough power between you. How can you ignore their cries, Joyce? Help them, dammit."

"Hannah's right," begins Mum. "We have to do something."

"We could draw the beast out to us," Galtonia suggests. "Away from the home."

"What?" gasps Joyce. "Then why waste time luring the beast into the basement."

"Do it. Please," I plead. "It buys the residents' time." I can't bear the thought of them being hurt or afraid.

"I'm inclined to agree with Hannah," adds Galtonia. "Draw it to us instead. We can handle it, Joyce."

"Don't you want to save your residents?" I cry.

Joyce screws up her face, "Of course, I do, but like I just said, this could get us killed. And I won't risk yours or Caroline's lives like that."

"Look, Eleanor is the strongest of all of us, but she's buried under half a tonne of rubble," says Galtonia. I don't appreciate the reminder.

Entering the conservatory, we crouch between rows and rows of coneflowers tall enough to hide us and still flowering. Mum, being an avid gardener finds our new hideout somewhat comforting.

"It wants me," Mum says all of a sudden. "So, if I really

am the bait, let me reel it in. I'll get to the car, making sure it smells my blood. I can lead it away while you protect Hannah and rescue Mum and as many of the residents as possible. But don't stay *here*." She looks up at the glass realising the danger. "This isn't at all safe."

"Mum, no! That's crazy. I can't lose you both! Please don't do this."

*I need to get through to Gran! If she could only hear me!*

I have to do something. This is just insane. I can't lose Mum *and* Gran. I won't let that happen.

"Your suggestion is most admirable, Caroline, but I cannot possibly let you. I have to protect ..." said Joyce.

"I know full well what you have to protect, Joyce."

It feels like everyone's building a jigsaw without all the pieces and I can't tell what the picture is.

"But her plan might work," interrupts Galtonia. "Isn't it worth at least trying? Think about it, Joyce. I will guard Hannah. You recover Eleanor. Caroline speeds away and the beast follows her. I'll conjure fireballs to blind it for as long as it takes to give Caroline a head start."

"And I know Norfolk's snaking roads like –"

"The back of your hand," I say, realising I'm fighting a losing battle.

"None of us know if Eleanor will even awaken or what state she will be in. The command has been given, Joyce.

We must obey it. Let Caroline at least try."

"Joyce, don't. Don't let Mum go. Please!"

But she just shakes her head as if the choices are in her hands and she can't tell left from right. *Maybe that should be wrong from right?*

I turn to Mum. "Please don't leave me. You can't."

*No! I won't let her.*

"I've got to try something, Hannah. Be brave. It will be okay."

"But you don't know that. It's a suicide mission! Mum, please!"

"If we're going to do this, it must be now, Joyce," urges Galtonia.

"Very well, Caroline, but I will escort you to your car then retrieve Eleanor."

"Retrieve Eleanor? She's not dead! She's not a body to be retrieved!"

"I'm sorry, Hannah. But I do want it on record, that I don't like it. I don't like it one bit," says Joyce ignoring my plea.

I slump to the ground. Mum's words echo: *'I have to try something.'*

Well, so do I, dammit!

# CHAPTER TWENTY-TWO

# Eleanor
### From the Ashes

*"Gran. Can you hear me? Gran, wake up."*

Hannah's words tap through the thick fog that clouds my skull, demanding attention. I cannot yet digest them, only pain registers. My ankle and at least two ribs are broken. Shallow breaths ease the pain only fractionally as my faculties return to register Hannah's words.

*"Gran, please wake up. I know you can hear me."*

I can tell how hard she is concentrating to make a connection, despite the physical distance between us.

She continues, *"I need you to wake up and hear me, Gran. Please, I'm begging you. Don't die. Please, don't die."*

I listen for a moment.

*"Hide, Hannah. Just hide."*

Even at this distance, I feel a tidal wave of relief swamp her. My empath powers were always the strongest of my gifts.

*"Please, Gran. If you can do something, then hurry. Mum wants to use herself as bait. She's going to get herself killed. The typhon will find us. Please, we need you. I need you, Gran."*

I sever our connection. Internally, I raise my firewall. I cannot allow any access. Not even Joyce at this point.

*How could Galtonia think Caroline's idea was a viable one?*

*Ruddy fool!*

But I will be the fool if I can't save my girls.

Screams and anguished cries echo down the hallway. I fear staff members will come looking for me and Joyce, endangering themselves. My only relief is that I am in the old wing. Surely, no one will look for me here? Maybe the nursing home wasn't the best haven for me.

Wincing against the pain as I inhale, I detect an aura around me.

*Hmm, Galtonia's cloak.*

I slide my hand across the cold floor gaining enough leverage to force myself up onto my side. *There!* The smoothness of the cloak slides against my head. I push it up and away, leaving it suspended nearby. It may come in useful.

Rubble falls from my damaged, tired legs as I will them to move. *Ah!* My ribs grate against my insides. All I can do is focus on breathing. I remain still for a second scanning the devastated room for something I can drain life from. My broken body needs healing and it's going to take more than a little houseplant for what I have to do next. I can see nothing of any use. Then, through the broken doorway a short distance along the corridor, a welcome sight greets me – an African violet – in a large ceramic pot, still intact. I inhale deeply, hoping for the scent of life. Dammit. *There are too many artificial plants in this place for my liking.*

Pained cries of residents fill the sky like stars, too numerous to count.

*What have I put them through?*

With Hannah's warning ringing in my ears, I feel the pinch of panic. I roll over onto my better side, easing the burden on my ribs and in doing so notice a pile of debris alight in the corner of what remains of the ward. A glint of red from the flames catches my attention. Close, too close, lies a fire extinguisher hissing. I need to get to the fire before the oxygen hits it.

"Gran! Quick. Mum and Joyce are crossing the gardens. They're running to the car!" Galtonia won't let me ... "

*How on earth has Hannah done that? Broken through my firewall!*

Even with this broken body, I will not allow that beast to take my girls or hurt anyone else. I begin to pull myself towards the cluster of flames, pushing the rubble from my path, dragging my useless leg behind me. I heave forwards reaching out to strangle the fire.

*Through ash and flame,*
*I shall rise again.*
*Through ash and flame,*
*I shall rise again.*

Flames pulsate through my body, scorching my blood.

*Argh!* Bracing myself, and with a steadfast grip, I wince and cry out as my hand burns black; the stench of my own flesh revolts me as it blackens and chars. My smouldering gown and robe disintegrate and I am grateful the fire is doing what it does best, spreading fast. I remain still whilst vines of fire curl around each limb. *Argh!* Both ribs crack back into place, the fire sealing the bone. Within seconds my entire body is ash-black.

Straining against the stiffness and pain radiating through my charred body, I lift the extinguisher and suck the oxygen from the valve. Its effects are instant. I snort out plumes of grey smoke. A surge of strength pulsates through every fibre in me. I slowly stand and shake the ash from my body. I look down at my arms; auburn and gold feathers – some with crimson tips, some with violet veins, reveal themselves. Every sinew breathes like a thoroughbred. I flex my back and unfurl my wings which sway back and forth with an eagerness I had long forgotten. I crouch in readiness, listening for the wail of the typhon. Finding my target, I take flight spiralling through the gaping hole in the ceiling. Thin streams of fire ripple behind me leaving a shimmering trail through the sky.

*A fiery death comes for you my friend.*

# CHAPTER TWENTY-THREE

## Joyce
### Firebird

"Caroline, wait! Not yet." My grip tightens.

The night is dark. Crouching between a fence and a line of conifers, we wait for clouds to cross the waning moon, before moving again.

"When the clouds are central, we go. Head for the back of the sheds by the car park. From there, we can weave between the cars."

"Joyce, do you think my mother will survive?"

"Yes." I lie because it is the kindest thing to do. She might.

"Can you still feel her heartbeat?" *I knew she would ask.*

"Well, not at the moment ..." Caroline clasps her hand to her mouth stifling a sob. "But that does not mean she is dead. Far from it, knowing Eleanor."

I feel Caroline's body fighting the sorrow that flows through it.

"Look at me. We're talking about Eleanor, here. Anything is possible."

She nods vigorously, swallowing cries that stick in her throat.

I track the clouds. Then, at the most opportune moment, tug Caroline forward. We navigate our way further through dense conifers and pine trees. Enabled by the damp undergrowth our escape is a near silent one. We reach the edge of a concrete pathway running out of the grounds, steadying ourselves to cross the car park unseen by the beast that bays for Caroline's blood.

*I wonder if she even realises.*

"Now," I mouth.

We run, never letting our grasp on each other slip.

A sudden gust of cool air wafts at our backs as a most welcome voice permeates my mind. *Anything is possible.*

*"Joyce, where is the beast?"*

*"Oh, thank goodness! Where are you?"*

*"Look up."*

*"Well I'll be damned …"*

Caroline and I stand and stare.

"Mum?" asks Caroline, her mouth agape at Eleanor's change of attire; she is nothing short of exquisite. Suspended mid-air, cast against the starry night, every human limb is adorned in close-knit feathers of firelight. Her red, lustrous mane cascades down her back. Her wings fill the sky, twitching with eagerness, clearly ready to surge. The moon begins to emerge from the clouds revealing a glint in her hawk-like amber eyes. A true firebird.

*"Yes, dear."*

Caroline's lip quivers as tears trace the apples of her cheeks.

"I thought you were …"

*"Shh. Now, now. All is well. Or, it will be …"*

*"Joyce, where's the beast?"*

*"The last I saw, it was heading towards the conservatory. We left traces of Caroline's blood there. It's using the buildings to keep as high as possible though. There's something different about this one. It isn't just banking on brute force. I don't like it."*

*"Joyce, you need to get Caroline into your car. Take the exit on the left and wait at the end of the lane. Ensure that not another drop of Caroline's blood reaches the air. I'm going to get Hannah."*

"Mum! Be careful," begs Caroline trembling and not from the chill in the air.

*"The police. Think of something to stop them. We can't risk fatalities. And the residents, Joyce. We have friends in there. Do something. Galtonia's cloak is still inside."*

*"I'll magnify its reach. It's expandable. You just keep that hideous creature to the east side. Oh and Eleanor … it's nice to have you back!"*

Suddenly – struck from the left – Eleanor hurtles towards the ground leaving a blaze of embers in her wake. Before I even register the presence of the typhon, Eleanor with her wings spread, swoops back up, missing an ambulance by inches. Caroline gasps, but before the scream surfaces,

I clasp her mouth, pulling her into one of the sheds. The typhon hasn't noticed our retreat.

*Oh Eleanor! Be careful, friend.*

# CHAPTER TWENTY-FOUR

# Hannah
### Britishness

It takes me a while to stop sobbing. I don't mean to be a baby, but I'm scared. Every question that marches towards me starts with *What if?*

"It is a very courageous thing your mother has just done, Hannah," begins Galtonia, throwing her arm around me as we shelter under a huge shrub.

Part of me agrees, but the other part of me thinks she's utterly stupid. Images flash of the typhon gaining on Mum, swiping the car in the air and it salivating as it stalks its prey. *No!*

"Maybe."

*I can't lose her. I just can't. And Gran …*

"I am detecting elevated stress levels, Hannah. Please calm yourself. All will be exactly as it should be."

*What does that mean?*

"I *should* be with my mum. I *should* be with Gran. But I'm sat under a mulberry bush or whatever the hell it is, with a stranger hiding from a beast that wants to kill us!"

"I can conjure some lavender if it helps?"

I shake off Galtonia's arm. I don't mean to be hostile, really I don't.

*I must calm down. I need to think straight. No lavender. No lavender required.*

"You can hold yourself with such restraint at times, Hannah. That is admirable."

"No, that's Britishness."

"Well, it is to be admired."

*Sometimes.*

"Huh! What was that?"

"Stay down, Hannah!" orders Galtonia pulling me away from the edge of cover, but I'm just not in the mood to take orders from anyone.

*My family's lives are at stake.*

A meteorite of blazing orange rockets across the sky, leaving trails of firelight.

*Wait a second …*

"Gran?"

# CHAPTER TWENTY-FIVE

# Eleanor
## Versus

Grimacing as the pain radiates down my side, I continue sweeping upwards. Despite being a little disorientated, speed remains my advantage. Time enough to establish a game plan. The typhon stomps across the grounds. I know it has eyesight like that of an elderly human, using its nostrils to navigate. I have to work to my strengths. The 20/5 vision I possess allows for much greater accuracy in tracking. Being down wind will allow Caroline and Joyce to sprint across the car park undetected.

*Grrawrrrrgh!*

*Dammit!*

Sniffing the air, the typhon halts, turning its thick head back. Glowering, it puffs out its ginormous chest and sends snarls to rip the air apart.

I charge instantly, wings narrowed. It raises its gargantuan arm, readying itself. I feel every particle of air against my feathers and skin. Its limb swings. I flick the fire-switch and feel the flames pulsate. My claws make contact with its scaly flesh, slashing its face to leave a deep burn mark in its flesh.

*Grrawrrrrgh!*

It leaps at my heels, but not high enough and slams back

into the ground. A sudden rush of emotion crashes over me.

*Hannah. Her fears threaten to devour her.*

I spiral up, curling round before coming to hover in the shadow of an oak tree and scan the grounds and hedges. Flicking from hedge to rock, car to outhouse. Every wind-kissed leaf that falls, every scurrying shrew or rat catches my attention. Eventually, I locate her. Sheltering under the extensive foliage of a Japanese japonica, I spot the contrasting colours of Hannah's jumper. Being camouflaged from the colour-blind typhon, I pray they remain still for their lives depend upon it. Behind me, I hear the light rattle of wheelchairs and beds – the remaining residents are being hastily evacuated. *Oh, thank goodness.*

It takes only a moment or two to cross the grounds and glide up over the half-decimated remains of the nursing home. I circle around the east tower, then aim towards the laundry block. Landing, my cloven feet grip the mud against the reverberating grounds, each of the typhon's thuds growing closer. I pant to cool my temperature, the glow of my wings fades quickly. *Less visible.* I move around the walls, staying close, flattened against them. Not easy, at this size, although still nothing compared to *that* beast. Playing hide and seek with a creature like this isn't easy. Concealed from sight, I study it as it crosses the gardens. It slows, sniffing the air. *Lost the scent it seems.* It disappears behind a high hedgerow so I take the opportunity to dart around to the front of the laundry block, feet skimming the grounds as I whip back in search of Hannah.

*"Galtonia, I'm here. Bring Hannah out."*

They emerge from the safety of the foliage, but stay close in case cover is required. Hannah's expression is priceless. Galtonia's, too for that matter.

*"Shh! I'm coming. When I say, run towards me."*

Galtonia takes Hannah's hand as I close in.

*"Now!"*

They dart forward, hopeful arms outstretched and I sweep low. *Gotcha!* I begin pulling upwards against their weight, but before I can make any headway, a huge shadow casts itself against the moonlight. I look to the roof of the laundry where the typhon waits. Its eyes flash, watching me, waiting for my next move. 'Gotcha,' they say.

I freeze like the proverbial rabbit-in-the-headlights and feel the weight of the decision I must make. Galtonia and Hannah dangle from my legs, their grips tightening around my claws.

"Gran, do something!" she cries. I glance down at Galtonia. Words are not necessary.

"Let go, Hannah." I relax my claws causing their grips to slide.

"What?" she screeches.

*She won't.*

I watch as the typhon eyes up my hindered position weighted down by loved ones. Galtonia looks across at the beast, before releasing her grip to grab Hannah who can't fight against the weight. They fall …

*Huh!*

Galtonia takes the brunt of it pulling Hannah onto her chest. They roll across the grass into the shadow of the crumbling building.

*"Be brave."*

*"But, Gran …"*

I sever the connection once more. *Focus.*

The typhon leaps high from one roof to the next, readying its strike. I criss-cross the garden and sweep up higher to keep Hannah within my line of sight. I push a wave of energy through my body, igniting the simmering flames until they burn bright. I whip around, creating a lasso and release it across the gardens. Landing, it encircles Hannah and Galtonia where they lay. *That should keep the typhon well away.*

"Who sent you?" I bark feeling the vitriol rise in my chest.

*How is this simple beast blocking me? A cloaking spell of some kind?* The work of the traitor Lord, whoever it is. Perhaps they knew I'd attempt to read its mind?

"A typhon beaten by a firebird. Hmm, it's a good job for you your brethren won't know your shame."

Growls rip from its chest echoing across the quiet of the gardens. It begins its approach. *If I rile it enough …*

"You were created in the darkness of the earth, and let me tell you, the earth wants you back!"

The typhon seizes the moment, lunging. I flit to my left, but it's fast. *Too fast.* Its thorn-crested arms slam into my wings as we crash together. *Ow!* It has been years since I've played with a beast such as this and have forgotten how solid their structure is. Feathers splinter and flutter into the night-sky. The beast moves again repeating the exact same manoeuvre and I counter, crossing my wings. Using a fire strike I send it thundering to the floor. *Payback.* It rolls smashing through the greenhouse, shattering the glass panels and decimating it. It remains on the ground for a moment, shaking its lump of a head. Its muscles flex as it stands; glass raining from its body. It pushes upward and I lunge. Our bodies smash together. We tumble and twist as if riding a rollercoaster, skimming trees, clutching each other, every strike more violent than the next. *I cannot let it wear me down. Ah!* A sudden sharp pain radiates down my limb as it begins crushing my wing. Immediately, I turn and peck its head dozens of times. Black blood spurts from its wounds, covering my face. Like a pecker bird, my beak stabs over and over until it lets go.

The typhon lashes out, slamming its fist into my back. *Huh!* My lungs snatch at the air. Its claws grapple at my wing, bringing a wave of nausea crashing over me as its claw pierces my scapular. We plummet and slam through the roof of the visitors' lounge.

Detached, I swoop away seeking refuge to gather myself, shaking the dizziness that hinders my senses. I check the damage inflicted by the beast, pull myself up and flex my wings to ensure no lasting damage, the wound stinging. Dust falls as my feathers ruffle. From across the lounge, the typhon begins bulldozing chairs and tables in its path. Cutlery clatters to the floor as the building shakes under the weight of the typhon. *Think, dammit!* I leap to the left as it swings around a pillar, vaulting the residents' piano; its slab-like thigh strikes out. *This typhon has speed like I have never seen before.* I take flight learning to become an artful dodger. My wings counter, steadying my suspension.

*Grrawrrrrgh!*

Hovering above a dining table, I focus entirely upon the typhon that wants to slaughter my entire family.

*I will not allow it!*

I watch as it sways its weight left to right, raising its palm to mop the blood still oozing from its pecked head.

*That's it!*

Suddenly, I lower my wing, leaving it limp. I lower my gaze, too. Bait. It charges! Leaving a whisker between us, I spring up over the beast and force a ripple of fire to cascade down my body, burning its claws which have targeted the wing once more. I slip through its grasp realising I have burned the pads on its hands.

*I despise being caged, like all birds do.*

Gliding across the decimated room, I break out through the patio doors sending the remaining panes of glass spraying into the air. Returning to the gardens, I taste the crispness of an autumnal frost setting in. In the distance, I see the glow of fire which encircles my granddaughter and Galtonia, the light smoke fills my minute nostrils. The beast quickens its pace to close in.

"Gran!" screams Hannah, but I daren't take my eyes from the typhon as I fight against a tidal of Hannah's fear for my safety.

"Enough! I don't know who sent you. I don't know whose bidding you're doing, but if I have to wipe every single typhon off the face of Gaian to find them, then, Gaia give me strength, so be it."

It lunges.

Power surges from deep within my core, my fire ignites. Springing up with speed to rival a peregrine falcon, I hurtle towards it. Thinning into a bullet-like form to shoot between the stumps of flesh it stands upon, I outmanoeuvre it, vault up and plunge my claws into its cold snake-like skin. Deep. Deep into its neck. It begins thrashing, trying to gain a hold as a fountain of blood spurts out. Arteries tend to do that. I send a surge of energy through my body, flames burst, dowsing it over and over.

*Ah!*

*Must. Hold. On.*

In a waterfall of fire, it begins to drown.

*Nearly…*

*Thud!*

Finally, the beast succumbs. A putrid stench rises from the hulk penetrating my nostrils.

*"From flesh to fire,*

*An earthly pyre you now lie upon.*

*Let your ashes scatter to her winds,*

*And may your shaded soul seek forgiveness."*

Life has forsaken it. The weight of the creature's death now rests upon my shoulders, even if it is a shade stalker.

# CHAPTER TWENTY-SIX

# Hannah
### Earthquake

"Gran, seriously, you are one scary old bird."

"Er, firebird. Not old bird, if you please. And I will try and see the compliment there," she replies as Galtonia conjures a thick custard-like liquid and dowses the ring of fire, smoke hissing as it rises up into the air. I dive into Gran's well, wings, I guess.

"Ow!"

"Sorry, Gran. You're okay, aren't you?"

"I will be. Just sore."

Her entire body is covered in the most beautiful flame-like feathers, which tickle the backs of my ears as I nestle in.

"And it is a compliment," I add.

"Well, that was … unexpected, shall we say," begins Galtonia. "Still got fire in that belly of yours, Eleanor."

Gran smirked. "Oh, what is it you young'uns say, it 'kicked my backside' there for a moment. Not as easy to defeat as I remember."

*Remember? Gran's fought typhons before?*

"Are you sure you're okay? I mean that looked *rough*," I say glancing up.

"I'll heal fast like this."

"This? You mean because you're from the cast of Sesame Street."

The eyebrow arches.

"Well, you'll have to stay like that for a bit because, er, hello, what happened to your nightgown?"

"Burnt to a cinder I'm afraid. Joyce will have something more suitable when we get to Windsor House."

"Unless you're planning on passing a Primarni, but I don't think there'll be one open at this time," I say glancing at my mobile. The battery is amber. *Not good*.

"Can I have my cloak back now, Eleanor?" Galtonia asks.

"Ah, yes. Came in handy that."

"So I see," says Galtonia glancing up at the remains of Willows Green Home, which looks like its wrapped in a huge blob of bubble gum.

"Is that your cloak?" I ask.

"Yes, but, it will spring back. It's lined with collagen, not cotton."

Galtonia double-clicks her fingers and I wonder what for. Then the nursing home starts to wobble like a giant blancmange, as the cloak peels back from the walls. As soon as it has, it begins folding in on itself, and after a moment, is, well, cloak-sized again. *Cool*. It glides across to Galtonia, who like a Matador, throws it around her shoulders.

"Yes, Eleanor, you *really* are quite scary at times. I had

forgotten just how much."

I'm guessing they don't get Sesame Street where Galtonia's from. *Where is she from?*

"Ah, so little time to bask in all these compliments."

"We'd better get to Mum. She's probably had a heart attack after seeing that thing. Has she seen you yet?"

"I think it was a jaw-on-the-floor kind of moment."

"You're on a roll then, Gran."

"Mmm, roll. I'm rather peckish, actually."

*Food, yes! I'd kill for cheese on toast.*

Together we cross to the car park. Mum and Joyce emerge from a shed. *Great hiding place!*

Mum gives me the once over then a huge hug before turning to Gran.

"Mum?" she begins.

"It's me, Caroline. I'm just the same as before," Gran replies offering her wing. Mum steps under it embracing Gran.

*Forgiven. Finally.*

"Joyce, what did you do to the police officers?" I ask.

"Simple. Lotus flowers and lavender. The Lotus induces temporary memory loss. Combine this with a heavy dose of concentrated, heated lavender, and well … goodnight officer."

"But how?"

Joyce, raises her hands then wiggles her fingertips before placing them on my cheeks. *Huh!* Hot!

"You could have burnt me, Joyce."

"Nonsense. As if I would do such a thing. What a notion. But my hands are very warm. It's just about working a little magic, that's all."

"You really are an alchemist. But, Gran, what about the nursing home?"

"Earthquake. Haven't you heard? There's been an earthquake in Norfolk. It'll be all over Breakfast News," she winks.

"Oh, really?"

Mum always said that I was far too sarcastic for my own good and now I know *exactly* who I get it from.

"But I meant the residents, Gran. Please tell me they're okay."

"I can feel every heartbeat in there. All 38 accounted for, which is quite extraordinary. Joyce worked her alchemy so everyone is fine. The lavender mist will continue to wind through the grounds and into every nook and cranny of that building."

"So, they'll all forget too?" I ask.

"Yes. And that is how it must be," says Gran.

"Unfortunately, a great many of these residents will already be in a state of no lavender required," Joyce says.

"What do you mean?"

"Dementia, dear. Most of the residents are here because of their dementia."

*So they won't remember anyway.*

My heart splinters at the thought. *How awful.*

"And that is why we chose it for your grandmother as a safe place to retire to, shall we say. Never recognised. Never remembered."

"But that's horrible!" I cry.

"I know, but necessary. Life isn't black and white, you know, Hannah," Joyce says.

"Right, well, we're not out of the woods yet as they say," begins Gran ruffling her feathers and actually wiggling her tail.

"Now what?" Mum asks.

"To the Hollow Tree," Gran replies.

# CHAPTER TWENTY-SEVEN
## The Unwelcomed Truth

Dusk weaves its way across the sky pulling a thick quilt of darkness behind it. We journey northwards from Norwich with Joyce trying to navigate the road closures due to the floods. She says being on some of the narrowest country roads, too many remain like streams so it's taking longer than expected, even if Mum does know Norfolk well.

The Hollow Tree sits in the grounds of Windsor House, a large estate and according to Joyce, not only is the architecture very grand, but the house has an extraordinary history. Before Joyce can continue, Gran interrupts.

"So, Caroline. May I?"

"Do I have any choice in the matter?"

Gran doesn't reply. She just stares at her own daughter blankly.

"I don't understand why she needs Hannah though," Mum says even before Gran begins. "Surely, she of all people can sort it out."

"I think *you* understand perfectly well, Caroline," Gran replies.

*Is Gran accusing Mum of something?*

That's twice she has done that today. Or, at least that's what it sounds like.

"Eleanor, let Caroline speak," says Joyce.

"I apologise. I understand your frustration. Really, I do, Caroline."

*Warning! Sarcasm approaching.*

"Oh, really? Well, I hadn't realised. Oh, pray, do tell."

I go to speak, but Gran raises her hand. "Joyce is right. We must let Caroline speak her mind. Clearly, she needs to get this off her chest."

"Y'think? So, you say you understand my frustration, but do you have any idea what we've been through today? What we've seen? What we've done?" I don't think Mum is actually asking us in the sense that she wants us to answer. There's a word for it.

*"Rhetorical."*

*"Thanks, Joyce. Please leave my head."*

*"Sorry, I really don't mean to, but sometimes dear your thoughts really are quite loud."*

Mum continues her ramble. "We get woken up at 3 a.m. to be told that you're dying; that you have just hours to live and that if we leave Yorkshire immediately we might make it in time to say goodbye. Then, I drive through the most horrific storm, end up crashing the car nearly killing me and your granddaughter after some … thing, well, attacks us. Then you terrify Hannah with your little ghost trick, the nursing home gets demolished by some creature from an 80s horror movie and then we …"

Mum loses her train of thought and sighs. She looks so exhausted. Perhaps too tired to be driving Joyce says, but Mum argues that if she drives it will stop her fretting. *Don't think that's really working.* I assume that Galtonia, not being from Earth, doesn't know how to drive and Gran, well she's shedding feathers like a December turkey.

"I don't like it. I don't like it one bit." Mum's found her voice again.

"It's not about likes or dislikes. It's about her destiny, Caroline."

My spine shudders. They mean me. Again.

Gran pulls her seatbelt out readjusting her position to allow her wings space to move. "There is much to tell you, Hannah. Much you need to know before we reach the Hollow Tree. So I will speak in truths."

And then I remember ... the Hollow Tree.

I meet Gran's gaze. "You're remembering aren't you?"

She leans over engulfing Galtonia who spits Gran's feathers from her mouth.

"You're working it out," says Gran.

I point at the feather-spitter.

"You said it. When you were with the Lords in the council room. You said to them the 'Potential' needs moving to a place of safety. I remember now. And you ..." I look across at Big Bird "... you had all this secret knowledge that you

164

were desperate to tell me before Mum found out. And then just before the attack that command … I have to be taken to the Hollow Tree …"

No one speaks.

Calculation face.

*How could I have not seen it?*

Silence waits patiently for me.

"I'm the Potential. Aren't I?"

# CHAPTER TWENTY-EIGHT

## The Elementals

Mum whispers something to Joyce about pulling over.

"No, keep going Caroline. We are exposed here and heaven knows what else may be out there. It's not much farther."

"Do you want me to explain, Hannah?" asks Gran.

*I don't know.*

I have no words which must be a first. My eyes fix on a tear in my jeans. Gran places her hand over it and begins. She's trying to fill the blank pages of my mind.

"The Almighty One we have spoken of previously, her name is Gaia. But humans refer to her as Mother Nature."

My jaw actually drops.

"Gaia tends to have that effect on many a being," adds Galtonia gently lifting my chin. I stare at her. "Yes. She's as real as you and I."

"And you, my sweet girl, are her living, breathing heir," begins Gran. "Do you know what I mean by this?"

Greedy gravity pulls me down.

*I'm gonna be sick again.*

Gran opens the window. I gulp down the fresh air and grab the door handle as if it was a life jacket and I was being tossed between the waves. I hear Gran's words and try to focus on her face.

"Do you understand what I mean, Hannah?"

It takes a while, but my breathing steadies as I attempt to process what she said.

I nod. "Like a prince to a queen; a bloodline."

"At present, you have an expanding ability to harness Gaia's gifts, her powers, just like the ones you're beginning to discover. In case anything should happen to Gaia, you would inherit, well, the world."

*"I can't breathe. Let me out. Let me out!"*

"Caroline, pull over. Quickly."

*"Thank you, Joyce."*

I yank at the seatbelt, releasing it and lurch out of the door. Five, maybe six steps, then my knees buckle, hands slamming into the tarmac. *Ow!*

*Breathe.*

*In. Out.*

*In. Out.*

There it is.

The truth.

I wanted it so much, but I'd never really thought about how I would feel when I heard it. Now, I wish Gran could take it back. Unwelcome the truth I'd asked for. I crouch on the kerb taking little shallow breaths.

"Hannah, sweetheart?"

Mum bends down at my side, curling her arm around my shoulders, squeezing me closer. "I'm so sorry. This is my fault. Mine, not yours. But you're going to be fine. We've got to get back in the car."

I've heard that phrase, 'you look like you've had the wind knocked out of you,' and I imagine this is exactly how it feels. I stare at the glistening grass verge. All I can think of is what it must be like to be a mole. I am suddenly jealous of their ability to burrow underground. *Why can't I hide in the deepest, darkest places just like they do?*

"Hannah, we have to go. Come on, love."

She takes one hand and brushes away the tiny pieces of tarmac that have pressed into my palm. Mum then lifts me up out of the roadside and takes me back to the car, where Galtonia stands holding the door open. In one seamless move, she begins the extravagant bow she had performed in front of the Lords.

"Stop! Don't. Don't ever do that in front of me again."

She moves aside, lowering her eyes. I don't feel bad for offending her because I can't feel anything. It's all just one big ruddy mess.

I climb back in and look down at my other hand. *I know something's there.* I peel back two, then three, then all four fingers. Pressed into my palm is the blossom of a quinine. I have absolutely no soddin' idea how I know that, but I do, and it's embedded into my skin. *What does that mean?* Gran and Galtonia join me on the back seat and I stuff my hands into my jumper rolling it up over my knees as I hug them into my chest. *Why does that keep happening?*

*******************

A quietness has filled the car, only broken by the occasional direction from Joyce. It allows Mum to concentrate on driving. In the back, I sit pegged in between Galtonia and Gran who refuses to let that vice-like grip of hers loosen. I wonder if she is listening to my thoughts. I can't explain why, but I want to keep them as quiet as possible. Maybe I'm scared. Maybe I've had too much new information stuffed inside my head. I rub my temples and decide that there isn't room for anything or anyone else at the moment.

Clearly, my thoughts aren't quiet enough though.

"Hannah, I know you don't want to hear any more right now, but there are a couple of things I must tell you and it cannot wait. Do you know what an element is?"

"Uh-huh. They do teach us stuff at school you know. Water, air, fire and earth."

"It's nice to know that your sarcasm hasn't abandoned you – always a good sign in my eyes. So, you'll know that each element is a special force."

"A force of nature."

"Yes, exactly that. Well, they exist in our world, in our

Universe."

"I know. I've heard of solar winds and stuff like that."

I begin to feel a little more at ease. The information I don't want to hear is actually helping distract me from the feelings I most definitely don't want to feel.

Gran explains that when we looked through the portal and watched the Lords and Galtonia, that there, that place, was Gaia's home. Is Gaia's home. Earth is its sister planet. I ask Galtonia what her home is called.

"Gaian, after our Mother," she answers.

"Gaia resides in Gaian, as you would expect, and the elementals reside here," says Gran.

"I know it's a lot to take in, Hannah, but you're doing so well," adds Joyce leaning back and patting my knee.

*Well at what? Not passing out? Not throwing up again?*

I replay Gran's words, then something strikes me. "I don't understand. The elements are all here. All four of them. Listen, can you hear me breathing? That's called air."

I can't help the sarcasm. Sometimes it feels really good to be really sarcastic.

Gran raises that HD-free brow of hers.

"The power of the Elemental Earth is equal to the combined power of Air, Water and Fire. When they are all together, their power is formidable. They are the most potent powers that control every ounce of life, as we know it. They can exist in the same world for a short time, but in order to maintain balance they are split equally in terms of their strength."

"That doesn't make any sense, Gran. We have all the elements here, right now."

"I apologise. I mean actual beings, Hannah. Like you."

"What?"

*Please let this be a dream. Or a nightmare, actually. I don't care. I just want to wake up.*

Gran looks at me pitifully, clearly listening. She sighs and I feel her hand clasp my chin as my head sinks. *"I wish I could read your mind, Gran. It isn't fair that you can read mine."*

*"When we have time, I'll teach you the art of reflection. It can block unwanted invaders, shall we say."*

Now that, I definitely want to learn how to do!

"Wait, does the Government know?" I have absolutely no idea where that came from! *Random or what.*

"No. And that's how it must stay," answers Joyce. "Can't have politicians meddling. They'd cock up everything for certain."

"Nothing new about that then," snides Mum.

\*\*\*\*\*\*\*\*\*\*\*\*\*\*\*\*\*\*

I keep my eyes closed, lulled by the motion of the car. So tired. And hungry. Had I known we wouldn't be eating for hours, I'd have swiped the rest of that packet of bourbons that Joyce gave us.

*Huh!*

"Hannah, what is it?" asks Gran.

I open my eyes and look at my hands covered in blood. I look at Mum through the rear view mirror, but her face is vanishing, fading. I lunge out to her and her body crumbles to ash and slips through my fingers.

"Argh!"

"Wake up! Hannah, it's a dream. It's a dream," soothes Gran. "You're okay. It was just a dream."

"Don't pull over, Caroline. Keep going. She's okay." I hear Joyce say.

Beads of sweat cool off making my body shudder.

"May I?" asks Gran. I nod. She 'goes' to check as the images of Mum's disintegrating body flash from my mind to hers.

"Oh my," she begins a moment later. "Now, now. Just a dream, Hannah."

I look at Mum's reflection in the rear view mirror. *She is there. For real, this time.* She smiles and I wish it could be summer again. Last summer we spent the holidays in Stratford, feeding ducks, watching play after play at the

RSC and eating enough cream and jam-filled scones to fill Buckingham Palace. I wonder if Mum is wishing the same thing as she does her, 'It will be okay smile.' I love our holidays together. Just us. We started the year the divorce came through and they've become our little family tradition.

I mouth one word to her. "Stratford."

The biggest smile spreads across her face, before she returns her attention to the road.

"Dearest, may I continue?" asks Gran squeezing my hand.

*No.*

"I suppose."

"Each of the four elements are controlled by beings who descend through a bloodline. Our bloodline. Each of them is a unique being. They inherit their gifts from generation to generation. It is not determined who receives which element, only Gaia knows that."

*A unique being? Each of them.*

What does that mean? That I have brothers and sisters? Family somewhere that I have never met? Questions approach, the rhythm of their boots is constant.

"Ah, we're here," says Joyce jumping out to open a pair of enormous iron gates that Mum has pulled the car up to. Inside each gate is a giant W. *Windsor House.*

"Welcome home, Hannah," she adds climbing back in.

# CHAPTER TWENTY-NINE

## Windsor House

We turn onto a dark narrow lane. The car judders crossing the cattle grid, before we curve onto a little sandy dirt track lined with what look like oaks and elms. I can't quite see how far the land stretches out on either side of the car. The length of the lane tells me the grounds must be enormous and I've lost count of the number of stately homes and parks we've visited since I bought Mum a membership to The National Trust for her birthday. *Took pretty much six months of pocket money, like.*

Eventually, we come to a circular driveway through another large iron gate. Mum takes the car round and stops near the entrance to Windsor House. It's enormous. Not the size of Chatsworth, but still. *Nice.* It is perfectly symmetrical, even the gargoyles which hang down below the floodlights are.

Gargoyles? Wait, didn't Gran mention those, something about Galtonia hating them, or something? I must admit they give me the creeps a bit. Joyce sees me looking at them.

"Don't worry, Hannah. Sinister they may look but the gargoyles ward off evil spirits. They are the guardians of Windsor House and will tell me if anything that could pose a threat to us is in the vicinity."

I laugh imagining the rows of mini foxes with their fierce, canine grins, the baby-sized griffins beating their wings and tails of the toy-like mermaids lashing around; each one screeching at her chipmunk style. Now I know this they don't seem so creepy. The house itself is beautiful and only the weather-worn grey slates tells its age. *I wouldn't mind living here!*

And then it dawns on me. "Aren't we trespassing, Joyce?"

"Well, you lot are, but I live here. Someone has to watch the tree."

"Are you kidding? You actually live here?"

"Yes, of course," Joyce replies.

"Then why doesn't Gran live with you? Why pretend she needs a nursing home?"

"Your grandmother is very powerful, Hannah."

"Now, now, there's enough of that." There's no hint of sarcasm in Gran's voice this time.

"We may as well answer her questions, Eleanor." Joyce turns back to me. "Because your grandmother emanates a certain level of energy, she needs to be reasonably close to the Hollow Tree, but if she were too close for too long a time, I mean days, weeks ... eventually, her presence could act against us. It would be like all the house lights being turned on during a performance of Swan Lake. The attention goes where the lights are. Speaking of lights, Caroline, if you can kill yours, please."

Somehow Mum and Joyce have established a quiet truce. I just hope it will last. I can't tell if Mum's forgiven Joyce for drugging her.

"Moonlight and floodlights will serve us just fine," adds Joyce. "And now, especially in light of what I've just told you."

"Won't the little gargoyles wave their paws and wag their tails at us if there was something wrong?" I ask.

"You're not funny."

"Yes, I am."

Gran says my humour is a welcome relief and pats my knee for being a 'chip off the old block'.

Joyce leaves the car, followed by Galtonia, who covers her head with the large velvet hood, feeling the October chill, clearly. *I left my hat in Mum's car.* They scan the gardens for a short while, then beckon for us to join them. Making our way up to the house, I can't help but feel a little mesmerised by the gargoyles that line the edge of the roof. I have a strange feeling Joyce wasn't actually joking about them.

Mum joins me, then says, "I know this is a silly question, love, but are you okay?"

I honestly don't know how to answer that so just shrug my shoulders and instead say the only thing that comes to mind.

"Bacon sarnie would be nice."

"Starving?" she asks.

I nod.

"Me too."

As we enter the house a strange sensation trickles down my back like sweat. It's a sort of familiar feeling.

"Mum, have we ever been here? Have I?"

"Yes. When you were very little."

I sense Mum wants to say more, seeing as there seems to be a new level of honesty between us, but annoyingly Joyce interrupts.

"What's the plan then, Eleanor?"

"Whatever it is, I hope food's involved."

Gran pauses and momentarily looks as if she is counting the tiles on the chessboard-style flooring. I see her eyes flick just for a second to Joyce who has sat down on the bottom step. *Private conversation?*

"We must take Hannah out to the Hollow Tree, but first we need to ensure her safety. Indeed, everyone's safety."

"What's troubling you, Eleanor?" asks Galtonia who has

been very quiet since I snapped at her for attempting to bow to me.

"All of it. Everything. I'm finding it rather difficult to comprehend. You see, to me, the idea that someone or something would betray Gaia like this is unfathomable. But not just that, I mean, really. It's preposterous. Who actually believes they can usurp Gaia. She *is* life. She *is* creation. It's absurd. Wouldn't you agree, Galtonia? After all she has given us, and I don't just mean planet Earth, but Gaian, too. Your kin are different in many ways to humans. For one, you certainly don't pollute the greatest gift that you have been given. But, I mean-"

"I am sure she will work it out, Eleanor," she replies. "If I know Gaia, and I do, this will all be resolved. And with the help of Hannah, of course."

"Oh, I have no doubt about that. None whatsoever. Gaia will survive this. And she will discover the traitor that lies within, if she hasn't already done so."

"Gran, if there's a chance it isn't one of the Lords that's poisoning her, then what else is making Gaia so sick?"

"Like I said, dearest, someone believing they could actually usurp Gaia ... I mean ..." Gran's steely glare flashes across us all. "They'd have to be ..."

"Pretty thick?" I suggest.

"Well, yes if the truth be told, but what is bothering me is the timing of all this. After all these millennia. Why now?"

"Eleanor, what are you getting at?" asks Joyce.

"What if there isn't just one traitor. One lone wolf ..."

"Go on."

"What if there are millions of traitors? Billions?"

The penny drops and I know it's landed on heads.

"Humans. You mean us, don't you?" I ask.

"Yes, I am afraid I do. Our climate is at breaking point. I've never experienced an environment as hostile as the one we've created. And it is our own doing."

"You mean the migration crisis and heatwaves," Mum says.

"Tsunamis, quakes, hurricanes. There've never been as many recorded in the last century as there has been in this, and it's barely begun," adds Joyce.

"What humanity fails to comprehend is that Gaia isn't just the creator, she is creation. Cause and effect. X and Y. Male and female. Action and consequence. Earth and Gaian. Two living, breathing biospheres until human inhabitants evolved and so began Gaia's demise," explains Gran.

"Her own creation working against her," Mum realises.

"Eight billion of them. Insolent usurpers," Galtonia snides. "Well, it would certainly make more sense, Eleanor. I mean her belief that a traitor lay in her midst seems, as you stated, preposterous. Maybe her belief was based upon nothing more than feverish ramblings."

"Yes, but we cannot rule anything in, and we certainly won't rule anything out," says Joyce passing a bowl of dates around as stomachs grumble.

"Why aren't we doing anything about it, then?" I snap.

"Maybe Gaia already is ..." Gran says staring at me.

*Am I her Plan B?*

## CHAPTER THIRTY

# 31st October 1821: Evelyn
### Favour

"Who's there?"

At the click of my fingers, the candle ignites.

"Come out of the shadows. I demand to know who is there."

I swing my legs from the bed, glancing back briefly to see William still sound asleep.

"Evelyn, it is I, Joyce," comes a whisper from behind the window.

Taking the candle, I breathe over it dimming its light, then tiptoe across the room. "Why are you here?"

"Not the reason you think. I promise you that."

"I don't believe in promises. You may enter."

The gargoyles lining the roof stay quiet, no cause for alarm as Joyce shimmers through the glass.

"Guardians still active?" she asks.

"Always. But they don't howl at old friends," I reply taking Joyce's hand. "It is good to see you again. It must have been …"

"At Caroline's enlightenment, I believe. Over forty years have passed."

"As much as I am delighted to see an old friend, I cannot help but feel much trepidation, Joyce."

"Your internal warning system has never failed you, Evelyn, so I know you will have sensed the change."

"I have, yes. And I have made my feelings very clear to her on this matter. I went to the Hollow Tree. I know Gaia will have heard me."

"Speaking of the Hollow Tree, Eleanor is moving the Potential there as we speak. There have been attempts on her life. I'm afraid we don't have much time at all, Evelyn. Will you extend to us what I know you will have already done here?"

"I take my guardianship very seriously."

"That is why I have been sent. Eleanor needs someone she can trust. Implicitly. And, with your lineage, Evelyn."

"Of course. Eleanor and Caroline are my blood. I would never refuse kin." I turn back to William to ensure he does not stir.

"Will you cast the spell across time for us?"

"I will do better than that, Joyce. Go back and begin the calling."

And with that, Joyce's astral self fades and vanishes.

# CHAPTER THIRTY-ONE

# 31st October 2021: Hannah
## The Calling

I can't believe how high the ceilings are. Hanging in the entrance is a huge golden candelabra, its candles only dimly lit. To the left, a wide, sweeping staircase runs around the cream and gold panelled walls. *Joyce lives in style!*

Whilst Gran has been in a deep discussion with Galtonia and Mum about the threat to Gaia, I have been staring at Joyce stuffing my face with dates from her fruit bowl. She hasn't moved. In fact, she hasn't moved for over four minutes. I know this because remembering I have my phone in my back pocket and grateful not even so much as to have cracked the screen, I note the time. 1:58 a.m. Now that mightn't have been unusual but for the fact that she literally has not moved. The only thing she appears to be doing is, well, breathing. I spit out the stones from the dates, one by one. Mum winks and takes the last two, clearly as ravenous as me.

*Has Joyce astrally projected somewhere?*

I am certain that she has and I bet Gran knows where to. That was the exchange I saw, that look Gran gave Joyce. That pause. A conversation hidden, I'll bet.

Where has she gone?

Gran is now by the window, her fingertips resting on

the sash as she peers out across the grounds. Mum and Galtonia are facing her, which means they can't see Joyce. Did Gran do that on purpose?

*"You've worked it out then, Hannah?"* echoes Gran's voice clearly tuning in to my thoughts. *"Someone's had their Weetabix."*

*"Someone would love some Weetabix. And, yes. Where's Joyce gone?"* My eyes plead, but she turns away.

"So you see, Galtonia. I do not doubt Gaia one little bit," says Gran switching between our conversation and theirs.

"And neither do I, Eleanor. Neither do I. What needs to be done now? What is our next move?"

*"Yes, Gran. What is our next move?"*

*Huh!*

"Joyce, you made me jump," I say as she takes my hand then Caroline's.

"Form a circle. Now," she instructs.

*Here we go again.*

"This, Galtonia, dear friend, is our next move," announces Gran.

That was weird. I mean, how Gran spoke to Galtonia then.

The circle formed, we begin as before.

"Hannah, please commence the calling," says Joyce.

"Me? But who for?"

"Yes, you my dear. Begin with her name. The calling is for Evelyn," adds Gran. Galtonia looks across at Gran a little surprised.

*What is going on with them?*

For a second I rack my brains, then it comes to me. *Light and sight.* I begin, "Evelyn, come forth into the light. Protected be upon first sight."

"Perfect." Joyce winks.

I remember them mentioning her name. Was she another, just like Galtonia? Each of us, in turn, recites the calling. Then the chanting begins.

Once more the tiny light appears. It is warm and glows russet like a sunrise. Gently swinging my legs to and fro, this time I enjoy the suspension as our feet leave the ground. *Still a bit jealous that Gran got to play Big Bird for the day. I'd love to fly.* A wave of warmth travels through my body like winter sunshine on a frosty morning. Then she appears. Evelyn. But I know less about her than I did on first meeting Galtonia. The light is bright, but soft. It encircles her and as it gradually fades, I see Evelyn in the flesh. *Another supernatural sort of being, I'm guessing, but more human looking. Like Gran, I suppose.*

Evelyn goes directly to Gran and holds her tight, lingering for a while.

"How strange to think of who we are to each other,

Eleanor."

"I am an old lady now."

Evelyn smiles. "We don't have long … shall we begin?"

"I think a minute to make introductions can be allowed."

"Of course. Forgive me."

"Evelyn, I would like you to meet Caroline. Again."

"Again?" Mum asks.

"Yes, Caroline," begins Evelyn. "At your enlightenment. You were just a baby when I last saw you. I held you in my arms and your little fingers wrapped themselves around my thumb and wouldn't let go. I thought I should keep you for myself."

Mum's jaw slowly opens.

"I need to sit down. This is a real … a rather … lot to take in. Excuse me."

I join Mum. She definitely isn't wearing her calculation face, more her WTH face. And she's definitely not in Automatic Bee Mode any more. *How can she be with Gran here?* Mum cannot take her eyes off Evelyn. Even though Evelyn is brunette and Mum blonde, their ocean coloured eyes are the same, their milky skin tone, too. Even when Evelyn speaks, she sounds a lot like Mum, especially when she drops our Yorkshire accent in favour of her 'telephone voice'.

"And this," begins Gran, "is Hannah. My granddaughter."

Evelyn looks astonished.

"Your granddaughter?"

"Yes, Evelyn. Our bloodline continues on," says Gran.

It takes Evelyn a moment to compose herself.

"Well, Hannah, is it? It is wonderful to meet you. I am, well, a relative."

"It's nice to meet you, Evelyn." I remain polite but struggle to hide my reaction. *Didn't she know about me?* Evelyn looks at Mum again with a sort of troubled expression.

*Awkward.*

Gran walks Evelyn over to meet Galtonia.

"What an unexpected pleasure," Galtonia begins. They begin a quiet chatter between them.

"Joyce, where's the loo? I'm busting," I ask.

"The downstairs W.C. is just round that corner."

"Do you want me to come with you?" asks Mum.

"No. I'm okay. Call of nature. Pardon the pun. I think."

Mum sniffs a little laugh. It's good to see her smile, even for a second.

*************************

A sudden flashback to the dream, the tree, the flood, losing Mum catches me short of breath. *It's okay. She's okay.*

As I pull the chain and wash my hands, my thoughts

turn to Evelyn. Our new arrival. I cannot get her reaction to me out of my head. The way she looked at me, then Mum. It was like she couldn't believe I even existed. She looked surprised. Like, really surprised. I hold on to the little basin, running the water. You see people in movies doing that. Like they want others to hear the water not the wee, or worse. I don't know if Gran or Joyce are listening to me. I hope not. Everything that has happened since that phone call woke me and Mum up seems unreal.

I look at my reflection.

What am I?

A Potential?

What the hell does that mean, anyway?

Seriously, how I can be the heiress to Mother Nature, I mean, Gaia? I'm so naff at science. I don't understand organisms and weather patterns and chemical reactions. That's all Mother Nature stuff, isn't it? Polar ice caps melting, global warming. What do I know about that? Surely, they have the wrong Potential? It can't be me. Or maybe it can't *just* be me. I know Gran said there were elementals, but she always talked about "them".

Plural. Think!

'The Potential.'

Singular.

I can't just be me, though. I mean, what if I'd never been

bor …

I turn off the tap, but something continues to drip.

*No. It can't just be me because what if I'd never been born?*

Without the flash-photography warning that people get right before cameras click, the day begins its slideshow. Mum's reaction to the claw mark. Her anger at the hospital. What was it Gran said … 'I think you understand perfectly, Caroline.' Then the typhon, glowering at Mum, finding its mark, smelling her blood. *Her blood.* Daubing *my* blood around the home, too. And all those little comments Gran kept making. Evelyn's surprise at my existence. I stare now at my own 'calculation face'.

Each flash-photo pieces together like a jigsaw to form an image.

*So, it wasn't just me.*

# CHAPTER THIRTY-TWO

## Abdication

I fling the door open. Gran and Joyce anticipate me. My boiling blood tells me this is more than just anger. Seething is a good word to describe the way I feel right now. I feel spots of sweat rise on my neck.

"Where is she? Let me past!" I can actually feel myself snarling.

"No, Hannah. I cannot, unless you calm down."

*Not likely.*

They shoot each other a look. "Don't you dare! Don't you dare discuss me like that again! I saw that!"

*"Lavender?"* Joyce's voice echoes around my head. I heard her! Jee-zuss! *I actually heard her.*

I regain focus. "If you even try to knock me out with a potion, I won't be responsible for what I do!"

"That is what worries me, Hannah," says Joyce standing firm.

"Your powers are growing," begins Gran. "And the fact that this is your ancestral home means you are becoming increasingly powerful. However, the extent of your power is still to be determined, but with great power comes great responsibility. And not just responsibility, Hannah, for you will carry such a burden, the likes of which you cannot comprehend, yet. So, I will not let you do anything you will later regret. Do not blame my daughter for this."

"Then who do I blame, Gran? You?"

"No one. Everyone. Who knows? Isn't that the problem with everyone these days? Whatever 'it' is, it's always someone else's problem. There's always someone else to blame. Now, *that* infuriates me. I will control your feelings if you do not make that choice yourself. But I urge you, Hannah, to make that choice yourself."

"Let her through, Mum. Hannah deserves the truth."

*I'm already up to my neck in truth. What damage can a little more do?*

I shove past them, breaking them apart. Instantly, I regret it, but I feel the rage churning in my stomach, rising into my chest making it difficult to breathe.

"So you're the Potential! It was never meant to be me."

I feel Gran's presence at my side.

"I was. I was the Potential. I am not anymore. You are, Hannah."

Evelyn steps to my side, taking my hand. "This is my fault, Hannah."

I rip my hand away. "I'm sorry, Evelyn, but this has nothing to do with you. I don't even know you."

"But you saw my reaction. I did not hide it as I should have. And now you are filled with fury and aiming it straight at your mother. Caroline is my blood too, as are you. And I will not allow this to break our bonds."

I look to Mum. "So, what? You couldn't be bothered? Didn't give a toss about your destiny or our family?"

"Something like that, yes."

"I get it. I understand now why Gran's so cross with you. How could you turn your back on your own mother like that? You chose Dad. And look how that turned out. You chose Dad over your own mother. How could you?"

"Because I wanted you more."

Truth swings a right hook, punching me in the stomach. Hard. Someone scoops underneath my arms and sits me down. Blood rushes to my head. I am completely floored. I guess the truth can do that to you.

"Hannah, Caroline chose to be a mother. She wanted a child. And *you* are that child. It wasn't a matter of choosing your father over your grandmother. She chose life. Your life," explains Evelyn.

"Hannah, I carry a heavy burden with me every day," begins Gran. "I should never have let her choice come between us. Now, that part is very much my fault. I just didn't believe your father was right for her. But I was wrong, because here you are. The result of that union."

"Shame that union didn't last. You were right about him," admits Mum.

"Right or wrong. That isn't important," says Gran.

Mum kneels in front of me, taking my hands in hers. "I'm so sorry I passed this burden on to you, Hannah. I hope you can forgive me. One day."

*Can I?*

The anger in me expels as the truth sinks in. I sit trying to work out which feelings are shouting the loudest, but I feel numb. Nothing. There is a pit of blackness deep inside. Then I hear them. Question after ruddy question demands my attention. I focus on breathing and trying to make sense of it all.

Eventually, I find my voice. "I don't understand what happened, though. Gran said I'm the heir to Gaia, but you're still alive. So aren't you the Potential, really?"

"No. I chose to abdicate. When you were little we came here, which is why you have a sense of the place. We went to the Hollow Tree and I gave my gifts to it for safekeeping, so they could be passed on. That is why it needs protecting."

I drink in everybody's expressions as Mum pours her heart out. All except Galtonia's. She remains by the window shrouded in her cloak.

Mum continues, "I just never believed, ever, that something would happen. I mean this is the real world, Han. Beasts and creatures and fairies, that's all nonsense – at least that's what I thought. Deep down, I didn't really believe your grandmother until I severed my gifts from my soul. After the ritual, I always lived in fear. I tried to forget it. Move on."

"Is that why Dad left? I mean really left?"

*Maybe Dad abandoning me is Mum's fault. Could it be?*

I wasn't sure and for even having that very thought I felt like I was betraying Mum.

"Maybe. Or maybe he's just a complete …"

"Caroline!" snaps Gran unexpectedly.

I don't know what Mum was about to say, but with the way she feels towards Dad, it's not hard to guess. I still wasn't sure how I felt about Mum passing the buck. And how I felt about *my* destiny. The March of the Questions, Symphony No.3 by Hannah Walsingham. *How do I switch it off?* Gran hears my thoughts and sends a haze of lavender over me.

*"Thanks, Gran. That helps."*

A smile curls at the corner of her mouth. It won't stop the questions, but it will stop me worrying about them all so much.

Joyce clears her throat, then reminds us why we are here and that we shouldn't keep Evelyn from her family for too much longer, which we all agree upon. Evelyn instructs Joyce to collect the five pillar candles from behind the hidden panel on the back wall of what was once her bedroom.

"They are still there, I take it?"

"Yes," replies Joyce. "Let us all go to the pentagram upstairs. It will save time moving all the carpeting and furniture down here for this one," she adds peeling a corner of a huge red and gold rug with her foot.

Mum takes my hand as we walk upstairs, but I loosen my grip and let it fall. I have so many feelings towards her right now. Part of me wants to run. I haven't run in what feels like forever and the grounds here are calling to me. I love being out in the woodlands amongst the trees. It always feels like I can run forever. I want to be outside in the fresh air, letting the chill of the night kiss my cheeks. I want to hear the crunch of the frost under my feet so badly. I guess Gran needs me to calm down as a second waft of lavender dusts my hair and shoulders. I inhale the scent and its affects.

*I have to learn how to calm down without needing the scent of crushed flowers every time I'm cross.*

I continue with the deep breaths. It definitely helps.

Once upstairs, the pillar candles are put in place at each of the pentagram points; Evelyn lights them in turn, all except one.

"Do you need the candles outside reigniting, Evelyn?"

"No, that will not be necessary because they are lit already, back home that is." It is strange to think that Evelyn's home is this one and that she has just come from there.

*How can the past still be living?*

"The internal light will work equally as well and like fire always does, it spreads. Seeing as you can't tear yourself away from the windows, Galtonia, would you please open one? The oxygen will act as an accelerator for the spell."

Evelyn, a look of such seriousness etched on her face, stands in the middle of the pentagram and asks each one of us to sit and hold the candle. Galtonia hesitates before joining us; there's something definitely off with the way she's behaving. I'm sure it's since we've arrived here at Windsor House. Maybe it's just tiredness and there's nothing all that different about her behaviour. How well did I really know Galtonia, anyway?

Sensing my lack of concentration, Evelyn 'ahems' in my direction, then continues explaining that with the amount of power that is flowing through all of us, it will create a spell ten-fold strong. She begins.


"The pentagram I cast out this night,
Protects our home beyond dawn's first light.
I am the Light Keeper. Hear my call.
Those who trespass, will wither and fall.
Through space and time and time and space
Cross through darkness to this place.

All Sacred blood, from this day forth
Protected be from East to West and South to North.
With Sacred blood passed into light, send this pentagram
out of sight."

Evelyn pulls a tiny dagger from her pocket, glinting against the candles' lights and draws a line of blood across her palm. The sting registers; she winces. I glance down at the trace of the scar that lines my palm; it tingles responding to the memory. The imprint from the quinine leaf has melted into my skin. Evelyn lights the last one. From candle to candle, she hovers her palm over each and blood drips into the flames. Suddenly, a crackle of light connects them all as a ribbon of fire and blood binds together and bursts out into the night. *Cool.*

A rush of heat ripples through my body causing an instant glow to my skin, before vanishing, leaving a light chill as the night air creeps in through the open window.

"It is done," she says.

# CHAPTER THIRTY-THREE

## Eleanor
### Chill

I throw a shawl over her shoulders, the weight of two worlds literally resting upon them.

*She is so young to bear this burden, but bear it she must.*

With Caroline accompanying Joyce for some fresh air and to do a little bit of 're-con' as Hannah put it, I feel some semblance of calmness for the first time since, well, a while. Hannah shuffles to rest her head against my lap as one of her legs lolls over the side of the Chesterfield. I think she called it 'chill' time. I will allow a few moments until Joyce returns with the all clear, then we must make our way to the Hollow Tree. Evelyn's protection spell is not something that can be broken, or broken easily – in fact, even I could not break it; such is the power of the Light Keepers.

Evelyn joins us and pats my knee, which makes me smile. "Hannah says that we are a family of patters; knee-patting, head-patting. Maybe, Evelyn, you were the first?"

"Alas, no. I remember my grandmother being a head-patter as a child, demonstrating a rarely seen public display of affection back then. Indeed, it is still rarely seen in my time. At least now, it seems people are unafraid to be affectionate. But being a patter is, most definitely, our side of the family."

"Speaking of family, Evelyn …"

"I will wait until Caroline and Joyce return and then I really must get home to my little ones and William."

"How is that fine husband of yours?"

"Very well, considering."

"He really is one of the good ones. A true gentleman. And, these days, a dying breed I fear."

"Really? Goodness. Not that William is perfect, by any means. But, I count my blessings."

"As I am sure he does. Are they all well?"

"I thank you, yes. Jack has developed a little selfish streak, but it does not remained unchecked. I think, perhaps, he is just a typical boy of his age. And stuck in between two very different sisters."

"I am sure Jack will turn out to be a fine young man. What are his prospects?"

"Our hope is that he follows William's footsteps in to law."

"Well, you can take comfort that Caroline has."

"Good to know."

"And Constance? She must be nearly sixteen."

"Yes. Not a girl any more, but not quite a woman, either. I do feel for her." Evelyn sighs.

"It has been too long since I have seen them all. You know, I am indebted to you. You have done me, all of us, in fact, a great kindness, Evelyn. I hope I can repay that kindness one day."

"We are family, Eleanor. So, let us hope you never have to. Your offer in itself is enough. Just protect this little one here," she says gesturing to the fair-haired bundle curled at my side.

"I shall, dearest. With my every breath."

"She is powerful, Eleanor and she hasn't even begun …" but before Evelyn can finish, Joyce's voice shatters the quietness surrounding Windsor House. I don't just hear her screams, but feel her heart rip apart.

"NO!"

"What? Eleanor, what is the matter?"

"Evelyn, protect her. I must go to them!"

And with that, I snatch a cluster of stems from a pot filled with ferns. I drain it of its power, unsure if it will be enough. Glancing back to Hannah, who being the light sleeper that she is, has awoken and bolted up.

"Gran?"

Her eyes beg me for answers. But I have none to give. I push my spirit out letting my body slump across the chair as I leave it. Hannah's guttural cries give chase. But I shut myself down, thinking only of Caroline and Joyce.

*I'm coming.*

# CHAPTER THIRTY-FOUR

# Hannah
### Traitor

I wrestle the blanket from my legs and run to Gran's side. Her body is still.

"Gran! Gran, come back!" Panic chokes me.

"She isn't in there, Hannah."

I remember the nursing home. The ghost of Gran floating in front of me, before I ran. All the feelings rush back. Fight it! I want to run again, to Mum this time, but how do I find her in this enormous estate?

"Evelyn, what the hell just happened?"

"I do not know, Hannah. Your grandmother shut me out before I could read anything."

"Galtonia?"

She remains strangely still, looking out of the window.

"Galtonia, what is it? Where's Gran gone?"

"It won't be long now."

Her voice has changed and there's a sudden familiarity to it I didn't hear before. Dread rushes like a river through me. I don't like this feeling. *I need you, Gran.* The training wheels have come flying off and somehow I'm meant to stay upright and not fall. But everything is moving too fast now and I can't think straight.

"Evelyn?" I ask, now uncertain of what I thought I knew.

She steps in front of me, unexpectedly, clutches my wrist and begins moving us backwards. Evelyn's chest is heaving, her eyes fixed on Galtonia, who slowly takes down her hood, unties the strings and lets her cloak slip to the floor.

A sudden piercing wail shatters the silent sky. I cover my ears, but it hurts so much I crumple to the floor. Evelyn grapples to pick me up.

"What is that?"

"The gargoyles."

"What? But that means ..."

Meteor-like thuds crash to the ground one after another. Looking out, I see at least half a dozen gargoyles smash to the floor, shedding their stone tombs. Each breathes and snorts. The huge foxes scrape their claws deep into the ground, their hackles high. A griffin, the only one as far as I can tell, wails and spits fire from its mouth, shifting its weight uneasily. Plumes of black smoke burst from its nostrils. *Not again! No!*

"They'll kill us, Evelyn."

"Not us. Her!" Evelyn puts her hands out to Galtonia in an attempt to block her.

"H-a-n-n-a-h," her voice curls around me just like it did in the car. "I need you, Hannah."

I remember those words that chilled my bones to their core. I remember the car spinning, the voice spiralling.

"I don't understand. That was you? In the car?"

"Of course. I'm surprised you didn't recognise my voice," Galtonia smirked. "I must be quite the, hmm, 'actress' is the most accurate human word I am looking for. Such a funny concept to us Gaians, people pretending to be whom they are not. I must admit I found it easier than I thought, just as he said I would."

*He? Who's 'he'?*

Evelyn keeps her flesh and bone barrier between me and Galtonia, but I feel the wrath rising in me and pulsating through my veins like never before.

"Do not react, Hannah. That is what this heinous dryad wants."

*Dryad?*

"Now, now, Evelyn. There's no need for that," Galtonia mocks. "I have not wronged you. Yet."

Galtonia begins moving ever so slightly, aligning herself as much as possible with me.

"Careful, Hannah. Don't play into her hands."

"Where is my mother? And Joyce?"

"Well, if my little friend, and when I say little, I mean enormous; if I think he has accomplished what I asked him to - what we sent him here to do, then your mother is dead." Galtonia's eyes flash red as she cocks her head to the side.

"Want to join her?"

# CHAPTER THIRTY-FIVE

## Jigsaw

"You lying witch! My mum isn't dead!"

*I can't breathe. No! This can't be real.*

"WHERE IS MY MOTHER?"

A voice booms around Windsor House making the windows tremble and I realise it's me.

"Dead. Her body is nothing now, but an empty vessel lain in a field that the earth will devour as it decays."

No. No. No!

*Gran, help us!*

I choke on salty tears that threaten to drown me. Evelyn pulls me back against a wall, but my legs can't take the weight that's pressing down on me. I slide down. I am empty. Contents drained. Packaging not recyclable. *If Mum is dead, just throw me away.*

"Come here and I will take you to her, before she is gone for good." Galtonia offers.

"Don't listen, Hannah. It's a trap."

But it might not be. What if the traitor is telling the truth? What if Galtonia has conjured some other creature to kill her? And why did Gran leave like that? I daren't even look at Gran's body slumped on the floor. I am suddenly full of fear of what Galtonia could do to it. I feel Evelyn squeeze my hand like she understands.

*My head and my heart fight and I don't know which to trust.*

I try to stop the sea of tears, but everything about me is stubborn, so why not them. *Help us, Gran! Help us!*

If I believe Galtonia, then Mum is dead. If I don't believe her, then she'll kill me and Evelyn right here and now. I sit in a mess of hair, my hair, not Mum's. Damp from my own tears. Not hers.

No!

I ball my fists and beat the wall behind me.

*Mum! Please don't be dead. You can't. You can't leave me. Dad left me. Not you. Please, not you.*

I hear Galtonia taunting Evelyn, between my sobs.

"Hmm, how pleased he will be when he hears. An orchestration even he couldn't have imagined."

Galtonia parades like a queen at a coronation, clearly delighted with herself, which makes the fury inside bubble up.

"And may I enquire, Galtonia, who exactly is this 'he' that you speak of?" asks Evelyn.

Galtonia chuckles, "Now, why on Gaian would I tell you that?"

"Well, I assume you're going to kill me so it's not like I could tell anyone. After all, I can't connect to Eleanor so it's not like she can read my mind."

"I could give you that pleasure, that inside information,

but alas, I am not at all inclined to do so."

"Sounds to me like you're not allowed to. You haven't been given permission. I admit, Galtonia, I am intrigued to know who your Puppet Master is. Who you've crossed over for. Who it is that controls you."

"I'm no one's puppet," spits Galtonia which pulls me back from the edge of despair and it doesn't go unnoticed by *her*. Her.

"Ah, I see we've calmed down."

*She couldn't be more wrong.*

"Stopped all that pathetic sobbing and wailing have you? It really is unbecoming, child. So, would you like to see your mummy again?"

Overwhelmed, I can't stop myself. I lunge forwards.

"Hannah, no!" cries Evelyn.

*Whoosh!*

A sudden wall of air wallops me, pushing me back to the floor. I skate across it, ducking to miss a table. Evelyn forces me to retreat against my will. Galtonia's shrill cackle fills the entire room. It makes me more determined, but Evelyn places herself between me and Galtonia once more and grips my wrist. Outside, growls and howls, snorts and wails of frustration vibrate down the walls.

*As if that will stop me.*

"Don't be foolish, Hannah," Evelyn warns.

I feel my cheeks burn.

*I'm not a little child.*

"Nice try, Evelyn, but do you seriously think a slab of marble or a chunk of wood will protect her once I've sent you on your way?"

Evelyn stands, but positions herself like a referee, watching both sides for the first move.

Sorrow has deserted me and I am filled with an overwhelming urge to rip Galtonia to pieces. I take in deep breaths, suddenly scared at my own reaction. Gran can't waft her lavender over me now.

*Breathe.*

*Breathe, you idiot.*

Crouched down, I scan the floor to see if there is something, anything ... there! Galtonia's cloak lies on the floor by the window. I realise now it must have been masking her presence from the gargoyles, a different sort of protection, I guess. *I need that cloak!*

"Sorry, Hannah," begins Galtonia, with a smirk across her face that I want to knock off with a cricket bat. "But the cloak is strictly on a one turn per customer basis and since its already saved your life once ..."

She suddenly curls her arms above her head, which sends the gargoyles outside Windsor House into a frenzy, like she is about to strike. Reflected in the huge gilded mirror, I can see the griffin charging into the walls. The house trembles, but little puffs of stone fall from the impact. Trapped outside, excluded from their duties, the foxes howl in pain.

*Can Gran hear them?*

I've tried calling out to her, to Joyce, to Mum, but nothing. I won't let myself believe Galtonia. It's a trap. I know Mum isn't dead. She can't be. She'd never leave me.

"I won't let you hurt her, Galtonia."

"But how can *you* stop me? You're just a Light Keeper, Evelyn. You don't have that power."

"I think you forget my lineage."

Galtonia instantly throws her arms forward, air her only weapon. But it is enough.

*Crash!*

Every pane shatters and showers Evelyn. She throws her shawl up to shield her face and curls down to the floor.

"Ah!" she cries as the glass rains down.

*I wish I knew how to turn it to dust like Gran had.*

Evelyn is hurt, and it's because of me! I have to do something, but I am already too late. Dozens of vines begin snaking in, through what is left of the window, their tendrils twisting around Evelyn. She immediately begins ripping them from her legs, but every vine flexes and contracts pulling tighter. She screams out writhing in pain.

*No! No! No! This can't be happening!*

"Evelyn, what should I do?"

But she shakes her head to answer my cry whilst I cower on the floor. I am not a coward, though. I glance to Galtonia who is conducting the vines like a symphony, engrossed in her own triumph once more.

Another chorus of wails begin. The foxes! Galtonia has smashed the window open. And they aren't outside the protection spell because they were part of the house when the spell was cast. They can get in!

Nerves ripple up my body, but I swallow them back down. Galtonia begins lifting Evelyn, almost mummified by dozens of vines, suspending her midair. The vines stop but hold her body in place as Galtonia begins a tirade of abuse at Evelyn and how pathetic she and Gran are, which makes my own hackles rise, but I force myself to refocus and dart for the window. Sticking my fingers between my teeth, I whistle as loud as possible. I was always the loudest whistler at school and it's finally come in useful.

Within seconds, the foxes swarm through the window, panting and snarling. In pads what I can only guess is the alpha of the pack. She is huge compared to the other foxes. *At least I think it's a 'she'.* All of them covered in thick silver-tipped black fur.

*Just like the foxes at the roadside!*

Seeing their eyes flash, I realise it is them!

Alpha stands at my side, but then lowers her body scratching giant claw marks into the wooden floor.

*Wait! Did they claw our car?*

I don't understand and feel a sudden confusion. What if they aren't to be trusted? Like Galtonia, the traitor. I look at Evelyn who registers my expression, but she doesn't know about the car being clawed.

"Aw, poor little Hannah. You look a little worried. What is going on in that fussy little mind of yours?"

I grind my teeth. "I don't think you want to know, witch."

"Really? Let me see if I can guess. You want to know how Evelyn can save you both. And if your little furry friends are truly powerful enough to beat me. Am I right?"

*My* furry friends?

I don't answer. Closing my eyes I touch Alpha and try to push my feelings out to her. If Gran is an Empath, maybe I am too. I hear a sort of huff sound and I know... her side is my side. She launches at Galtonia, who flies up and grapples at her fur, but Alpha kicks her hind legs out, sending the traitor smashing to the ground. The other foxes leap up and begin devouring the vines, tearing them from Evelyn's body. The griffin, too large to get in, stalks around the house, snorting and whinnying, slamming its horse-like hooves into the ground.

Alpha and Galtonia fly apart, but as they do, Galtonia

pulls a dagger from her cloak and slices the air, catching Alpha's snout. Her cry cuts through my heart.

Freed from the vines, Evelyn plummets, but the foxes break her fall. She slides off them, clearly relieved.

"Thank you," I cry, briefly stroking one of them as I rush to Evelyn's side freeing her from the last of the lifeless vines, which are now scattered across the entrance hall. The pack forms a breaker between us and Galtonia, as their leader tracks her every move, step-by-step. She brushes herself off, a look of disgust on her face.

"Dirty little scavenger."

*Gran was right.*

It's then that I hear a whispering sound. I look to Evelyn who, eyes-closed, is chanting the same words over and over again, but so low I can't make them out. Like a painter, Evelyn's arms, make brush-like strokes through the air. Over and over and over again.

What is she doing?

"No!" Galtonia cries distracted by Evelyn's skywriting. "Don't you dare!"

But Evelyn clearly dares.

From the corner of my eye, I see Alpha spring across the room and pin Galtonia to the stairs. I'm sure she's going to rip her limb from limb, but she just presses all her weight onto Galtonia's chest, who gasps for breath. Alpha presses a paw against the traitor's throat, her claws sinking in. Thin lines of blood trickle down the side of her neck.

*She bleeds like us?* I don't know why I am surprised, but I am. Maybe I expected it to be green or something.

Evelyn then slowly rises from the floor, her arms sweeping the same shapes but her movements grander than before. I can't help but expect some great creature to come flying in at us, or bright light blind us, but she stops and reveals a hand-drawn shape, with fire-tipped curved edges the size of a windscreen suspended in the middle of the room. Beyond it is darkness. Nothing but darkness. The shape itself looks as if it has been drawn by a sparkler against a November sky. Evelyn takes my hand.

"Hannah, I need your power."

Grasping the centre of the oval, she pulls it away like a cotton sheet being stripped from a bed. I stand staring for a moment at the dark space left there, like a jigsaw-piece has been ripped away from a picture puzzle of Windsor House. *This can't be right.* But then a sudden whirring begins.

"Evelyn, what is that?"

"I call it a jigsaw, but your grandmother calls them Hollows."

*Seriously?*

"Lethal, they are," continues Evelyn. "If we were outside, I'd create a vortex, but they would suck the life out of whatever crosses their path. Jigsaws are easier. Big or small. It really does not matter."

Evelyn looks across at Alpha pinning down the traitor, surrounded by her pack. One approaches Galtonia's face, dribbling saliva as it sniffs her.

"Get off me you filthy beast!" Galtonia snarls.

"Evelyn, what exactly does a jigsaw do?"

"Many uses. This one will send her into the dark realms of the universe. And there she will stay. At least, that's what I hope."

With a bounce, Alpha pushes her weight down onto Galtonia's chest which takes her breath away. She splutters before crying out. "If you think you've won, Evelyn then you're a fool. Thanks to you and Hannah's dead mother, I know everything."

I bristle.

"How dare you talk about my mother?" I won't allow myself to believe a word she says.

"Oh I dare. And to think I had to bow to you! But it matters not, because we will destroy the Hollow Tree and he will come back for the old crone and you," she gestures at me. "And the bloodline will be erased from the face of this earth."

Alpha heeds the threats, her coat changes colour to a deep shade of red, as she slashes an enormous pad across

Galtonia's face, imprinting her claw marks upon her cheek. Her coat changes colour!

"No, Alpha!" I cry out. "No. That's wrong. Even for a piece of scum, like her."

The pack howl in disapproval at their leader being told off, but one bark from her, silences them all. She bows her head, her coat returning to silver, clearly knowing I'm right but I do appreciate the defence, more than she knows.

"Alpha, if you will do me the honour of depositing our guest through the jigsaw," begins Evelyn. Alpha grips Galtonia's arm, squeezing her jaws tight, ready to fling the traitor into the darkness, but what happens next, happens in a blur, like the world is opaque leaving nothing as it should be.

# CHAPTER THIRTY-SIX

## Alone

"EVELYN!"

But I am too late.

I barely knew her, but she is my family. She protected me.

And, she's gone.

The moment Alpha yanked on Galtonia's arm to throw her through the jigsaw into the darkness, Evelyn had readied the piece which was meant to seal it again. But Galtonia – clutching a stray length of vine discarded by the pack as they freed Evelyn – lassoed her, pulling Evelyn through with her. I can't get the fear in her eyes as she faded into blackness out of my mind. I throw myself at the space where the jigsaw hung, fingertips search for anything to grab onto, to pick at, but there is nothing.

"Evelyn! Evelyn, come back. Come back!"

I crumple to the floor once more, sobbing. I cannot bear this.

*I can't breathe. What do I do?*

My whole family is being extinguished before me. Cries to Gran remain unanswered.

*Why doesn't she hear me?*

I am alone.

Through a glaze of tears, I sense movement. Alpha and

her pack nestle around me. I look to her, their leader; dried blood encrusted onto her snout. Blood she spilt protecting me. Light from the chandelier catches Alpha's eyes which radiate a silvery-blue warmth, framed by her long eyelashes. I realise her entire coat is tinged with blue. I understand her anger being red. But what does blue mean?

I'm not even sure if Alpha is a she, or not. Not that it matters.

*Will Alpha understand if I ask?*

I point to myself. "Girl." Then point to Alpha. "Girl."

A sort of snort spurts from her snout, Alpha's head nods, then she shuffles forward and her lolling tongue scrapes up my face.

"Girl, then."

*Yip, yip.*

Alpha. Girl. *I like it.* I push my hands into her silvery-blue mane of hair.

*Schlump.*

Her tongue is rough against my cheek. Another tear falls.

*Schlump.*

She waits patiently for more.

Maybe I'm not alone, after all.

## CHAPTER THIRTY-SEVEN

### Fire with Fire

I wipe Alpha's kindly-meant slobber from my face and pull myself up from my knees; the room spins. Alpha whimpers and nudges me again and again; her wet nose brushes my hand. One of her pack has settled, curving its body protectively around Gran.

"Whatever happens, you stay here, okay? Never leave her side. Do you understand?" The violet-eyed fox nudges my hand. *Yes.*

Gran looks peaceful. Like she's sleeping. But, the thing is, she isn't sleeping. She astrally projected.

*Maybe her energy level has drained and that's why she can't respond. Or, maybe Mum is dead and Gran can't face telling me the truth.*

There are just too many 'or, maybes' so I stay focused on the one that makes most sense. She's low on energy.

'*Your mother is dead. Want to join her?*' Galtonia's words suddenly echo down the corridors in my mind, taunting me.

*Shut up! Shut up! Shut up!*

A sudden prick of heat surfaces across my skin. I try to breathe through it, but I can't.

'*Your mother is dead.*'

I picture Galtonia's sneer. The look of a traitor's triumph, short-lived as it was. I'm shocked by the change in how I feel. The pack have already reacted and have all moved back, all except Alpha who hasn't left my side, but her coat flickers from silver to amber.

I'm suddenly too warm. Sweat pools in my collarbone and across my brow, but this is no dream I can wake up from, like before.

*Want to join her?*

Galtonia's face re-emerges and I see that flash in her eyes. Traitor.

I grab my chest and try to steady my breathing, but I can't stop this feeling. I want to find Galtonia and tear her limb from limb.

*Oh God, what's happening?*

Suddenly, billowing smoke rises all around me. Alpha retreats.

*What's happening to me?*

I roll my sleeves up, noticing the changes across my hands and arms. My veins, like little blood-filled rivers glow and move underneath my skin. A strange burning smell fills the air.

*Is that ... me? Whatever is happening is happening and quick.*

A sudden need for air strikes me. *Let me out.*

Fire always needs oxygen.

I rush to the door, throw it open and gulp down the air. In front of me stands the griffin.

*Get a grip, Han. Calm down. Focus. Family. Find them.*

"Will you help me, Griffin?"

It bows and then rears up letting out a whinnying cry, slamming its hooves back down. I think that means yes.

My craving for air grows. My legs twitch.

Alpha and her pack of foxes pad to my side and together we run, Griffin at my back.

\*\*\*\*\*\*\*\*\*\*\*\*\*\*\*\*\*\*\*\*\*\*\*\*

We tear through the forest. Branches and thorn-filled bushes scratch my face and arms. *More battle wounds.* They sting, but then wither at my touch, their embers fluttering up into the night sky. I don't understand what's happening, but I can't think of anything else except getting to Mum.

*Please let her be alive.*

*Please.*

Racing through the woodlands, dodging oaks and elms, I feel fear closing in. Fear that Galtonia spoke the truth. Alpha stays the closest. I feel safer with her at my side. I leap over the stump of a felled birch tree. Crunched branches snap under our pounding pads and feet. After a short while, our pace slows a little and a soft breeze carries the smell of burnt wood to us. Trails of scorched thickets lie in my wake.

"I don't think that's me."

Alpha snorts and we head further north from the house. Trampling over exposed roots and thick grasses, the foxes leap with ease, whilst Griffin and I now struggle through the density. Frustrated, Griffin leaps to my side. Taking the scruff of my jumper it throws me up onto its back. Griffin puffs out a small line of fire, clearing a pathway. The river of red underneath my skin is beginning to fade. We travel on, leaping over felled pines and ducking under the low hanging beech branches. Soon, the smell of burnt wood is replaced by something new – something revolting.

*We're close.*

Great thuds vibrate through the damp ground shaking the ancient woodland. The foxes slow and Griffin, carrying me, follows their lead as we enter a clearing. My eyes dart across the darkness at every little sound.

*Where is Mum? She has to be okay. She has to.*

But it's too quiet. I don't like it. Then, from the corner of my eye I see Gran inside a dome of light. I whisper to Griffin and we dash forwards. Alpha and her pack spread out forming a running circle around us.

A deafening crack ricochets over my head. I follow the sound and see Joyce. Thin daggers of what look like ice shoot from the palms of her hands as she stands at the highest point of a small ruined hut. I look to the skies but can't see what she is aiming at.

But I hear it.

*Whumph. Whumph. Whumph.* I've heard that sound before. Wings. Whatever it is, it's got wings.

"WHAT ARE YOU DOING HERE?" bellows Gran from her protective position. "And why on earth did you let her leave the house?" She glowers at Alpha who lets out a sorrowful howl.

"Where's Mum?"

Gran shifts slightly and in her light, I see Mum's scuffed boots, her still body, her blonde hair straggled amongst the grass, her face, peaceful. I fling myself down at the dome of light, placing my hands against it.

No! I don't believe it. Galtonia was telling the truth!

And suddenly, it's as if I have been scorched; the scarlet fire I had almost extinguished rockets to the surface. Rage accelerates from deep within the well of my stomach. I look towards the sky, before glancing back at Gran who greets me with a look, half horror, half pride.

"What is that thing?"

"A draconite. Fire breather."

I realise I don't care.

It killed my mother. *It has to die.*

Joyce sends more daggers of ice surging high up towards the beast. Slowly, I stand and turn towards where it now circles; licks of fire shoot out of its cavernous nostrils. I can hear nothing except the rush of blood. Light from the autumn moon gleams against the serrated weapons it proudly displays as it snarls at Joyce. The draconite's eyes are ruby red, each one easily the size of my head. The creature's granite-like scales, which cover its lizard-shaped body, flex. It extends its wings; their span stretching out across the clearing.

I *should* want to run and hide.

I hear Joyce ordering the foxes, 'Silverbacks' she calls them to protect me, but they already understand that their place is at my side, not in front.

"Stay and protect my family," I say.

Three tail off, one to Joyce, two move to Gran and Mum, but Alpha stays just close.

The draconite sweeps back and forth higher into a sky littered with stars. Joyce fires another round of ice-like daggers at the creature, which impact, then fizzle into nothing. I spot a cluster of moss-covered boulders.

"Alpha, can you give me a boost?"

She lowers herself and I climb up onto her back, then with a nod, Alpha catapults me up. Losing my footing as I land, I grapple with the sharp edges of a boulder. Eventually, I pull up and stand staring into the sky and into the draconite's eyes. Alpha stays low, scratching the damp earth eagerly.

"What is Hannah doing?" Joyce calls out to Gran.

"Beginning to believe," replies Gran. I hear her words.

I suppose I am.

"My daggers aren't doing anything. There's nothing to extinguish its fire. Make it rain so I can mould it to ice," suggests Joyce frantically, but her cries seem lost on Gran as we exchange a look I know she understands. I realise then her power has drained, but she won't leave Mum's side.

"Eleanor, did you hear me? We need something, anything. *Cry* me a weapon for goodness sake."

"Water will not kill this fiery beast."

Even my voice sounds scorched.

"What do you mean, Hannah?" asks Joyce.

The challenge rips from my chest.

"YOU FIGHT FIRE WITH FIRE."

# CHAPTER THIRTY-EIGHT

## Eleanor
### Alive and Dead

Holding its skyline position, the draconite sneers at Hannah, indignant that a little girl dare challenge its might. It begins beating its wings, each stroke more powerful than the next. Its backdraft sweeps across the clearing, but it only fans her flames. I turn to Caroline and hold her wrist between my fingers. *Slightly stronger. Thank goodness.*

A ferocious snarl bursts from the draconite's slavering jaws, shaking the ground beneath us. Alpha responds to the challenge, but her barks and snarls cannot compare.

I immediately release the block I'd put in place and tune into Hannah's thoughts. The block I had put in place to protect Hannah had shielded everything.

*Evelyn!*

"*Galtonia betrayed us, Gran. And I don't know where Evelyn is. I lost her.*"

I flick my empath switch and am floored with wave upon wave of Hannah's feelings, one after the other. How is she still standing with all this flowing through her? I am astounded and realise it is too much. I have never felt power like this from another. I don't like it.

"*Hannah, listen to me. Your strength comes from the Hollow Tree. That Hollow Tree has stood on this earth since the dawn of time. It is rooted here, as a sacred place. Your name is Walsingham for a reason and it has been so for over a thousand years protecting the bloodline's true identity. The Hollow Tree is sacrosanct and will only bestow its gifts to one who holds no hatred in their hearts, heiress or not. The Hollow Tree will serve you, but only from a place of light. You must defeat this creature, Hannah because I cannot. But choose. Light or dark."*

She circles her foot back, shifting her weight.

From its suspended position the draconite rears up, its roar ripping the sky with a battle cry I have heard one too many times before.

Hannah shudders, looks at me, then to Caroline's lifeless body.

From its chest and up its throat, a sea of fire glows from under its skin. It spits fire from its nostrils as it begins its descent, fearing nothing. Certainly not a little girl and her pet fox, even if the fox is as large as a lion. Its coat undulates between a bright claret and a deep amber. *Warning.*

Following Joyce's lead, Hannah extends her arms. Sparks of white fire begin to crackle and ripple down them. Gone is the anger from its light. It's cooler, but more luminous.

*Angel.*

*"Thanks, Gran."*

*"Returning the compliment, I believe."*

She heard me! Truly, I am astonished.

The draconite, so immense in size, slows at the treetops now, close enough to scorch all those beneath it.

"You killed my mother!" Hannah calls out, but, extraordinarily, I don't detect a drop of hatred in her heart.

It snorts understanding her perfectly, and now seeking her death.

*I can only wonder on whose orders. Who shaded Galtonia's heart against us, against Gaia?*

Hannah releases a huge swathe of cool fire; her aim surprisingly accurate, but then draconites are difficult to miss. The fire fills the clearing above a cluster of oaks and elms, but fails to reach its target. She needs more power.

I grab Caroline's cold, limp hand, then hold my hand to the sky summoning the air, channelling it through our bodies. Momentarily, Caroline's body, filled with energy awakens. Oxygen fills her eyes, her arm raises, sending a surge of air across the clearing hitting Hannah square in the back. Generations connected, she casts her arms out before her, as our oxygen feeds her reins of white fire striking the draconite in its chest. Just like I had, Hannah circles her arms, creating a lasso, but its length still isn't enough to wrap around the draconite's neck. The beast, merely shakes off the attempt, but retaliates sending a shower of flames towards her. Alpha springs up, knocking Hannah from the boulder and out of the line of fire. Hannah tumbles, dazed, as Alpha lands out in front of her, but Hannah drags Alpha back against the boulder to shield her and begins brushing the embers from Alpha's singed fur.

As the oxygen dissipates, Caroline's body slumps to the ground, her glazed eyes fix upon me. I close them and fight back an avalanche of pain.

The draconite rises higher re-positioning itself. Its scales glimmer against the cool white of the moon. Hannah is in desperate need of more power.

*Think, woman. Think!*

I try to tune into the beast's stream of thoughts. It has realised that this little girl it beholds has not the power to broach the distance it has set.

"Gran, how can I get it down? I can't reach it!"

The draconite lets out a cry as if to sneer jokingly. It clearly has the ability to comprehend our language.

*A multi-lingual draconite? I've never heard of such a thing. Galtonia's doing, I bet. I dislike all this tampering with the natural order.*

Then a most ridiculous idea springs to mind. I would have to bait it. If it saw me as a threat, it would need to descend in order to wipe me out, meaning Hannah could lasso it. It means showing my face and leaving Caroline exposed, but what else can I do?

*"Joyce, I'm going to bait it. If anything happens to me, get*

*Hannah to the safety of the Hollow Tree. Promise me, Joyce, you won't let anything harm her."*

*"I've got a better idea. I'll be the bait. She's your granddaughter, Eleanor. Don't leave her again!"*

I know she is right. There is no point in arguing with Joyce, who has a streak of stubbornness that rivals my own. And so I let my dearest, oldest friend step into a literal line of fire in place of me.

Being almost a slip of a girl at 69 human years of age, Joyce strides across the clearing throwing everything she has at the draconite. It rollercoasters round, before soaring down after her.

"I hope you know what you're doing," she calls to Hannah.

So do I.

# CHAPTER THIRTY-NINE

# Hannah
### Defeat of a Different Kind

I suck in air through my teeth, calling her. Griffin doesn't keep me waiting long. Soaring majestically, it glides across the treetops unnoticed by the draconite. Joyce darts through a maze of boulders, as it bears down on her.

"Silverback?" I whisper.

One of the foxes approaches.

"Take this to my grandmother." I place Galtonia's cloak, which I'd snatched before leaving the house, in the fox's mouth.

"Hurry."

It nods, then pads away undetected.

I cannot believe the size of the draconite, but its size is something I will use against it. Too big to notice the little things, I guess. Well, I'm little. But I think it's time it noticed me.

As instructed, Griffin launches to the skies and the foxes charge at the draconite's lower limbs. Spotting the silverbacks, the draconite leaves what is left of the decimated boulder which Joyce hides behind. It begins great pendulum-like swings with its tail, striking at the foxes, who scratch and bite its legs. Alpha circles it repeatedly, much to the draconite's annoyance. I dart to

Joyce, cowering under a globe of light, her only protection.

"Are you okay?" I ask.

She looks exhausted.

"I will be. What do you need me to do?"

"Weave through the woodland round to Gran. She's guarding Mum's body. I can't lose Gran, too."

Joyce looks confused for a moment.

"Oh, and Gran has Galtonia's cloak."

"I will do as you ask, Hannah. Are you sure you can kill this beast by yourself?"

"Who said anything about killing? If I really am who they all tell me I am, I must wear that label. And that label is nature. The Mother of *all* nature. I probably won't ever be her and I can't say I want to. I'm not a mother, of course. I'm way too young for that, but I'm female and Mum says we hold the power of life itself deep inside us. She also said, that if ever I was lost or in need, that I should always rely on my instincts, my gut instincts. And killing isn't an instinct I have, no matter how I feel about what it and Galtonia have done."

Joyce touches my cheek, her eyes fill. "The world is lucky to have you, Hannah. I will do exactly as you ask."

"Thank you, Joyce."

She gives me her orb of light, kisses my cheek then vanishes into the trees. For a moment, I wonder which one of them is the Hollow Tree. Surely, if I speak to one of the trees, I speak to all of them. They are all connected families themselves, after all. No different to us. Maybe that's part of their beauty; what we love about them.

*"Hollow Tree, I am here to ask for your help."*

Knowing I have very little time, I rest my hands on a nearby tree. From the fissures in its bark, I know it's been around a while. From the hairy branches and purple-black buds, I can tell it's an elm.

*"I know you can feel me because I am certain I can feel you. Every stem, bud and branch. Every hidden root that gives life. I get it now. And I was wrong. Fire cannot overwhelm fire. Bestow your gifts upon me and I will use these gifts, not as weapons, but as instruments. I will use them as they are meant to be used."*

The tree shudders. Instantly, roots burst from the ground piercing my skin and begin pumping water through my body. Cold, but cool. It doesn't feel like drowning, more like my body's swimming without the ability to touch the ground. As the water settles, I feel it lapping inside my body. *Good job I don't get seasick.*

Okay. Here goes.

"Where are you beastie? I want a word with you!" I cry.

Emerging from a parting in the trees, I glance to see Griffin upon the draconite's back, striking it, forcing it

231

lower and lower, beating its impressive wings with every ounce of strength it has. *Lower, Griffin, lower.*

Great cries full of frustration rip from the draconite's core.

Somehow I know exactly what to do, like I've downloaded an internal app that guides me every step of the way. My arms extend upwards and I push the water through my body and down my arms releasing just enough to create a lasso. Then, as I aim to harness the draconite, it begins ...

*Pit-pat.*

*Pit-pat.*

A single tear of rain hits my hand and trickles down my arm.

*Pit-pat.*

*Pit-pat.*

*Pit-pat.*

Clouds release their heavy burden and rain tumbles to the ground.

*Thank you!*

The lasso's now sapphire thread entwines around my arms, bleeding its brilliance into my skin. I watch the silverbacks leap repeatedly for the draconite's legs. It swings them to and fro avoiding their snarling jaws. Tirelessly, Griffin slams its weight into the beast as it struggles to fight under the weight of the rain.

I stand, drenched.

Then, run.

Charging with every atom of energy I can muster, I leap up and lasso the draconite's limbs. Alpha and her pack grapple for the length of the lasso which dangles down. With our combined weight we begin dragging it downwards. It bucks violently and flings us all from it, but it can't stop the rain from extinguishing its fire. I brush myself off and launch again, silverbacks at my side. I throw the lasso once more, gripping tightly. One thing's for sure, I'm no cowboy. I swing on the rope as the pack yank harder and harder. With one last almighty shove from Griffin, the draconite is floored. It lays in a pool of water, fire-less and power-less. The rain eases to a trickle.

The silverbacks surround it, clouds of cool breath pluming from their jaws. Alpha stays at my side. She is so loyal and I never once asked for it. *Wait! Maybe that's it!*

Griffin perches upon its conquest proudly. An exhausted plume of smoke billows from the draconite's mouth. It huffs and sighs, defeated.

I pull wet hair from my face and move towards it, crouching close. I am sure it could still kill me if it wanted to; its mouth full of weapons too numerous to count.

Gran's voice echoes across the clearing, warning not to trust it. But I am overwhelmed with a need to protect it.

Those feelings simmer from deep inside, although I'm not really sure why.

*Is this how Gaia feels?*

I touch the draconite's thorny face; it flinches.

"Shh."

Eventually, it sighs, its battle lost.

"I will not hurt you even though you have hurt me and mine."

I stroke the side of its cheek, tracing my hand around its eye, which must be the size of a bicycle wheel.

"The rain will stay until every flicker of fire has been extinguished once and for all. Then you are free to leave. And you leave with your life. Which was a courtesy you did not bestow upon my mother."

Its eyelids drop. I know it understands me.

"Hannah, your mother is alive!" whistles Gran's voice from across the clearing.

*"What?"*

I daren't believe it, but feel a river of relief ready to burst.

*"Truly, she is alive!" adds Joyce.*

Then suddenly I hear it.

*Thump-thump. Thump-thrump.*

*"Put your hands on the ground, Hannah."*

*I feel it! I can feel Mum's heartbeat.*

*Thump-thump. Thump-thump.*

I have to see her.

Griffin snorts, reminding me that a gigantic beast lays at my side awaiting its fate. I turn to the draconite.

"My mother lives. Her death will not stain your soul for the rest of your days. I will give you your freedom, but if you take it, you must swear your allegiance to me from this day forth. And in return, I will offer my loyalty and protection for you and all your kind. I will keep this vow if you pledge allegiance to me and me alone."

*"Well, I never,"* came Gran's voice.

*"Alpha gave me the idea. It's her you have to thank. And, I figured we might need them one day."*

Through its weariness, the draconite raises its head and nods, then bows, closing its eyes. I place my hands upon its huge temples. I feel its heart just like Mum's.

*Thump-thump-thump.*

*Thump-thump-thump.*

Griffin gently lifts from the defeated beast's back.

Reading my mind, Gran sends a large, highly potent lavender mist across to the draconite. It drifts off to sleep, as Griffin, the silverbacks and Alpha run at my side.

*Mum!*

## CHAPTER FORTY

### Entombed

I stand staring at the stillness of her body, her mouth slightly open. *Always slept like a goldfish.*

"Mum, wake up." I kneel at her side, my heart pounds as the light rain trickles through my hair. "Why won't she wake up, Gran?"

"I don't know, Hannah. It might be ..."

"We have to get her to a hospital, then. What are you waiting for?"

"No. Somewhere safer."

"But she'll die, Gran. What are you playing at?"

"She won't die."

"What do you mean?"

"She *can't* die."

"Of course she can't. I can't live without Mum. Please Gran, she needs a hospital. Now."

"Not that sort of *can't*. She is not vulnerable to the weaknesses of normal humans because you and your mother are not 'normal' humans. Your bloodline hails from a higher power. From Gaia."

"I don't understand, Gran. Are you telling me we can't die?"

"Oh, you can die, alright. But not from human frailty."

*What?*

"The draconite struck her with its tail," begins Joyce. "Hard, too. The brute force knocked her out. But not in a human sense."

"I really don't understand this," I reply.

"I think your mother's natural instinct kicked in when she was injured," adds Gran.

"What does that mean?"

"Well, when threatened, a human will go into 'fight or flight' mode."

"And?"

Gran continues, "We are different. Do you remember when you were out cold after the near-miss with the car?"

I nod.

"Well, because of our nature, our gifts, we do not go into a coma like a human might if they survived an impact."

"Are you telling me, Mum's in a coma?"

"Not quite, but I suppose it's the closest thing I can describe it as. You weren't in a coma when you were unconscious. Your consciousness moved to a place of absolute safety, which is why it was so easy for me to, well, 'visit' like I did when I entered your mind."

Questions return ... stomp, stomp, stomp, bearing down on me. And this time, I'm not afraid to ask.

"Why aren't we rushing her to a hospital? Gran, if she dies ..."

"Our coma-like-state is similar in that it is like a self-preservation mode. A coma can be a means to recover from something like a severe brain injury. But, not everyone recovers from them. If people do recover, it can take weeks, even years."

"What are you telling me, Gran?"

"Your mother has gone to her place of safety."

"Then go and bring her back."

"I can't."

"What? Of course you can."

"Don't you think I haven't tried? It's like a computer uses a firewall."

"Has Mum done the same?"

"Yes, but she's blocked everyone out. Neither I nor Joyce can get in. But you managed, somehow, to break through mine. So, there's a chance."

*I can't believe this. Mum has locked herself away. I have to try. She'll listen to me. I'm her daughter.*

"I need to try."

"Hollow Tree first."

"No, dammit. Mum first."

"For this, you won't have the power without the Hollow Tree. My consciousness was here, within earshot. Who knows where your mother has gone to? You need your mother's gifts that she gave it for safe keeping if you're to

238

stand any chance at all of breaking through into her mind. She has blocked me, all of us. Maybe not willingly, but she has. She doesn't even understand the art of reflection, but it appears she has used it to retreat to her point of safety."

I look from Gran to Mum. How do I choose?

"But I'm her daughter."

"And I am her mother, Hannah."

I wouldn't accept that Mum was dead and I can't accept this.

"Then get me to my tree so I can try. I won't leave Mum trapped somewhere. Whether she's blocking us on purpose or not. I need her, Gran."

"I need her too, sweetheart."

I am fed up of surviving. It feels like the entire day has been just about surviving. *How do people do this for even more than one day?*

"Hannah, we have to entomb your mother's body. It's still vulnerable. It is best if we hide her away. We cannot leave her exposed," explains Joyce.

It's strange but I know she is right. A few days ago, I would have been a brat and argued until I was blue in the face, which is laughable now because I probably am blue in the face if the rest of me looks anything like my hands. I know I have to do everything I can to protect Mum until I can find a way to bring her back.

Alpha slaps a paw onto my leg. I place my hand on top of her paw. Alpha's breath is warm on the back of my neck. I nuzzle my face into her wet fur. I'm tired and want nothing more than to snuggle into the safety of her and dream my way to Mum.

*Where did she go?*

I hear the rest of the silverbacks and Griffin settle around us.

"Ah, no. Don't get comfy, we must return Caroline to the house, now," says Joyce to our new friends. "But, may I take the opportunity to thank you. Thank you all for what you have done for us."

Carefully, Griffin kneels down at Mum's side. Clasping her jacket between her teeth she pulls Mum's limp body up. Gran and Joyce help me lift Mum onto Griffin's back. I place her head gently against Griffin's mane. I stay at her side, warming her hand. Gran wraps Galtonia's cloak around me. I'm not sure how I feel about wearing the traitor's cloak, but Gran reminds me of its powers and that those powers now rest on the right shoulders. *Stomach flip.*

"Here, Eleanor. Take this," Joyce smiles pressing a thick bunch of ivy into Gran's hand. "You're one tough old bird, but you'll be needing this. And plenty of it."

"Thank you, Joyce. How would I survive without you?"

"I have absolutely no idea, Eleanor," she grins.

With the rain subsiding to a drizzle we set off back to Windsor House.

************************

As we walk, I explain to Gran everything that happened with Galtonia and Evelyn. She expresses her disgust at Galtonia's betrayal and wonders which of the Lords it is who she referred to as "he." She tells me she held her suspicions about Galtonia, but lacked proof of any betrayal. I tell her about the jigsaw Evelyn created and can't help but tear when I think of where she might be. Joyce says that she will contact all the Light Keepers she knows of and will ensure Evelyn makes it home. It makes me wonder if someone will do the same for Galtonia, meaning she's still out there and a threat. But I guess there's nothing we can do about that now.

As we enter Windsor House, Joyce sends a warm gust of wind through the reception clearing all the vines and glass into a single pile.

"Can't have our new friends splintering their paws, can we?" she says, before instructing Griffin to keep Mum on her back a little longer.

Immediately, Joyce begins removing furniture, but not with her actual hands. Using the air again, she pushes large pieces of furniture into corners of the room. Gran helps, twirling her fingers to begin rolling up the largest rug I have ever seen. It reveals the rest of the pentagram that Evelyn showed us before we began her protection charm. The pentagram covers the entire floor of the reception. Its lines of emerald green and gold mark out its shape against the sandy marble floor. Gran says that it is not as extravagant as the décor seen in the High Council's chambers, but I prefer it.

Entering the middle of the pentagram whilst Joyce lights the pillar candles, Griffin slowly and gently kneels down. Alpha steps forward and helps Griffin lower Mum's sleeping body to the floor, even taking care to place her head with her paw.

"She'll be cold, Gran." I can't leave Mum like that. It's not right. I can't bear to think of her suffering.

"No, she won't. Wait and see. Trust me, Hannah."

With the candles all lit, Joyce kneels down close to Mum.

"Almighty Mother," she begins. "Here lies your daughter, Caroline of the Walsingham line – your line. As only a mother so benevolent can, encompass her in your light, envelop her in every protection you can afford until such time as she is ready to reunite with us. Anchor her spirit from where it rests to this sacred place, this house of worship, binding her forever to it, forever yours. Conceal her being from those who would trespass and seek this daughter out. Continue to protect your bloodline, mother to daughter, daughter to mother. This we ask of you, Almighty Mother with hearts filled of everlasting light. Blessed be upon this night."

Joyce nods to each of us and Gran repeats her words.

"Blessed be upon this night."

Gran looks to me.

"Blessed be upon this night."

The pentagram groans as it begins moving, each slab of stone breaking apart to reveal a kaleidoscope of lights and colours that swaddle Mum like a newborn baby.

"Mum!"

Grief threatens to pull me down but being the Empath that Gran is, she realises and pulls me in close to her chest, feeling everything I feel, I am certain of it.

"I can't stand this, Gran. I just want her back. It's all my fault. If I'd just gone home when she told me to, she'd still be alive and we'd be together." *What have I done?*

I want to dive into the light with her. I can't bear her not being with me. I struggle for breath convinced my chest is caving in on me.

"Mum. I love you!"

I look at her face as the pentagram begins pulling her down.

"No! No, Mum, don't leave me." Gran clutches me, but I pull away and rush to the edge of the light. Alpha's teeth sink through my jumper dragging me back, whimpering.

"Mum!" But her body vanishes deep under the marble floors of Windsor House. The candles flick and fade.

I understand now how people die of a broken heart.

Even with Gran, Joyce and Alpha at my side, a griffin and a pack of silverbacks to protect me, I have never felt so alone in my life.

# CHAPTER FORTY-ONE
## The Importance of Trees

"I didn't know there were so many different kinds of trees."

"And each and every one is vital to the existence of life and nor do I mean just human life. There are wondrous gifts of life who were here long before we were and will be here long after. All species rely on trees or plants. From the deepest coral reefs to the mountain alpines," says Gran.

It hasn't taken us that long to walk from Windsor House into the woods where the Hollow Tree sits waiting. Gran insisted that I wear the cloak until I had been through the "gift retrieval" she said.

"Joyce will protect Mum won't she?"

"With every fibre in her being. You know she will."

It was hard saying goodbye to Joyce. She'd saved mine and Mum's lives and protected Gran. And now she was left alone with the most important job I could think of: protecting Mum. Alpha had called two more of her pack, who had broken free from their stone tombs which lined the roof of Windsor House with dozens of other gargoyles sat silently waiting to be called. She instructed them to protect Joyce and Mum at all costs. Before we left, Joyce invited Griffin to stay, too and so she wanders around the grounds keeping watch. *Mum's little army.*

"Hannah, we are here."

Alpha and her pack each pass me and nudge the back of my hand. I love the feel of their silver fur and even the odd wet nose isn't too bad. Together, they settle onto the grass with Alpha keeping closest to me.

I look around the small clearing at all the different trees and wonder which one is the Hollow Tree. I must admit, I thought it would be enormous and floodlit, or so different to any other tree I've seen that it's obvious which it is, but then that's just stupid, isn't it?

"It is time," says Gran.

Goosebumps spread across my arms as a tingle skates down my spine. Gran turns towards one particular tree, but its set back in the shadows and even with dawn approaching, it is hard to make it out.

"Hannah, since the very moment life was created, it appears there has never been such a threat to its existence. This threat is not a singular spearhead anymore; the apathy of mankind, but an intended, targeted threat from a traitor who lies within our realms, but remains unidentified. Its duality has the ability to dry every drop of life that has ever fallen within our common universe with a voracity the likes of which have never before been witnessed. Our Almighty Mother's gift, so given to us in good faith and benevolence, is being defiled and destroyed both consciously and unconsciously. Annihilation by the treacherous hand of one, extinction by the ignorance of many is a reality we must now face. Our Almighty Mother has been struck down, poisoned and polluted. So, for the sake of all life, a Potential has been called."

Gran takes my hand and leads me closer to the Hollow Tree. I can't help but smile. It's an oak tree, still dressed in autumn gold which catches against the lowering moonlight and emerging first rays of the daylight.

"I offer this one being, who holds the will to make amends and renew. An awakening must be realised and this Potential readied should the unspeakable come to pass. For she will inherit all, and it will be incumbent upon her to choose to continue life for all."

*I can choose? No. Surely, not!*

That single thought terrifies me. My stomach plummets through the ground. Alpha whimpers detecting my distress, but Gran ignores it. No lavender required.

"Kneel, Hannah Walsingham."

A sudden glow of light begins radiating from within the tree. Now within touching distance, I can smell the sharp scent of its bark, like a conifer. I'm desperate to trace the deep crevices with my fingertips. My eyes drink it all in. Every delicate branch sways, stretching its limbs like a ballerina. With its soft, bright canopy of glorious golds and sun-kissed browns you can barely tell it's nighttime.

"Thank you for the rain," I whisper. A branch curls down and strokes my cheek.

*Huh!*

*Flash!*

The dream. The flood. Open branches reaching out to catch me.

*Flash!*

Gran begins again, and I'm pulled back to here, now.

"Hollow Tree, I present the heir. Behold in her the bloodline we are sworn to protect. Awaken from your slumber and welcome the Potential into the Sacred Circle. It is time."

"What exactly is the Sacred Circle?" I ask.

"A circle that is sacred."

"You're not funny, Gran!"

"Yes I am, dear."

Gran instructs me to move to the very base of the Hollow's trunk and place the palm of my hand against it. Startled by a tiny crackle for a second, I swear I can feel a heartbeat which grows and from behind my palm as a thin line of white-gold traces up and down in between my fingers to the base of my wrist. It tickles. The glow pulses as it grows stronger, radiating out from my handprint. I watch how the Hollow Tree's branches flex, swaying back and forth, and each leaf flutters like a thousand cocooned butterflies emerging from their sleep. My touch seems to have caused a reaction.

*"Chain reaction,"* whispers Gran.

From deep inside the trunk, light seeps out from every crevice. The further it moves, the brighter it becomes creating a wheel of light like a geisha's fan. I glance at Gran who remains outside its light.

Gran picks up my trail of thoughts.

*"I am not a Potential. This light is not meant for me, Hannah. Just you."*

"Look, Gran!" Mesmerised by the four little balls of light which have appeared, I am engulfed by a feeling that I wish I could describe, like happiness and peace bundled into one.

"Sprites, sweetheart." *So pretty.*

The sprites spiral around me, flashing every glorious shade of green.

"The Hollow Tree is your source, Hannah. Your heart is at its core. And its core lives in the deepest realms of your soul."

I hear Gran's words and register them, but I can't take my eyes from the sprites as they unravel what looks like a silkworm's thread creating the most delicate looking chain of light. With every flick and spin the little wisps tinkle like Christmas bells.

"Hannah, hold your hands out," calls Gran.

I take a deep breath, struck by a sudden thought which makes my stomach flip.

*"What if the fire comes back, Gran?"*

"It will, darling. But you have nothing to fear."

How I felt towards Galtonia scared me. I don't ever want to feel like that again. That much anger inside one person. Nothing good ever comes of that, does it?

I trust Gran, so refocus back on what the Hollow Tree wants to show me. Light continues to illuminate the Hollow Tree's deep russet and gold branches which stretch wide and reach high.

*Is the tree growing?*

Each branch is covered in delicate olive and emerald leaves creating a lush, velvety canvas against which the most exquisite rubies and aquamarines blossom. Peaches and plums, ripe and juicy hang low glistening with dew.

*I want to bite one.*

Every vein of life that breathes from the tree is tipped in silver and gently pulses each time the Hollow Tree exhales. It is alive! It really is alive. A cluster of long-limbed branches scoop underneath me. They cradle me as I rise up.

*Just breathe.*

*It won't drop you, idiot.*

It feels a little like when Joyce began the 'Calling' and we rose up from the ground. Pearl drops, like rain, shower me in sapphires and jades, vibrant violets and every colour of red you can imagine. I glance down watching a metallic deep peach-coloured liquid seep through my hair. My eyes flutter against the invasion of colours I'm surrounded by.

*"It's too much, Gran."*

I press my hand against my heart, gulping down air and open my eyes and see dozens of hand-shaped twigs, some with knuckles like buds, layering leaves across my body, stitching together a gown of green. My hair now dances around my shoulders and skirts my cheeks. Pulling a strand between my fingers, the dull blonde has been replaced by a rose-gold glow, strands of lime thread plaited through it.

*Flash!*

I picture her. The other Hannah – my future self. It's more incredible than I remember. She said the dream was real and it is. It really is.

*Flash!*

*Incredible.* I know this is no Disney cartoon, but I feel like Belle, just not in blue.

*"I wish Mum could see this."*

*"I will teach you how to send her your memories. She won't miss it. I promise, I will."*

*"Really? We can do that?"*

*"Of course!"*

*Maybe that will help her wake up and bring her back to me.*

I suddenly feel like someone has poured a spoonful of hope down my throat. I look around at Gran, the forest, the moon and sky, the Hollow Tree. *My Hollow Tree.*

I begin to sense everything changing in me. Everything seems clearer, brighter, and more real than reality, if that makes any sort of sense. I can taste everything in the air, feel every drop of air as it bumps against my skin.

"One final thing, Hannah. Empathy. My gift to you. There are traces of it already within you, more than traces, in fact," begins Gran. "Of all the gifts I can give you, this comes the most naturally to you, so I shall merely enhance it."

The Hollow Tree lowers me to the ground. I can't help but smile looking at the dirty, scuffed boots on my feet, while the rest of me looks like Cinderella on her way to the ball. Stumbling to the edge of the sacred circle of light, I struggle lifting the weight of the gown. I stretch my arm out, crossing the line of light. Gran touches her fingertips to mine. A sudden surge of energy rushes through my body, tingles, then fades.

"I feel like I can fly, Gran! Although, in this, I imagine that would be pretty damn difficult."

"We don't say 'damn' dear."

I pull my 'oops' face.

"Today, a Potential was born. I declare Hannah Walsingham, the one true heir of Gaia, Mother of all Creation."

I sigh and try to catch my breath. "Any chance I can do that again, Gran?"

She laughs. "I think once is quite enough."

"The tree is so beautiful. But then I think all trees are beautiful."

"That's because you see them through the beauty that lies within your heart, Hannah. You have surprised ... no, astounded me. More so than any other being I have met in these last hundred years."

"You're a hundred years old?" *No way!*

"Well, there or thereabouts."

We fall to the ground laughing.

It feels so good to laugh again.

# CHAPTER FORTY-TWO

## White Gold

We lay on the ground right at the very entrance to the Hollow Tree, staring at the stars, hands clutching tightly. That's so cool, seeing the stars through the trees.

"Gran, do you think Mum is up there somewhere?"

"Possibly, yes. Maybe not in that exact star, but yes."

"We must find her."

"We will, my darling."

*I know Gran won't stop until she's found a way to bring Mum back to us.*

I can't wait for her to teach me how to send my memories to Mum; wherever she is, she won't ignore them. She'll find a way to wake up and come back to us if Gran doesn't beat her to it. The panic and pain I felt at her not being there with me, always close, or just at work, or just at the shops, has definitely eased since the Hollow Tree bestowed its gifts upon me. Which were Mum's, actually. So I guess, now even a larger part of my mum is locked inside me, forever making it easier to breathe knowing she is just somewhere else and not gone forever.

"Well, we have a very good chance now the Hollow Tree has imparted its gifts to their rightful home," says Gran.

"I can feel it, you know. The Hollow Tree, I mean. It's feeding all the trees around it. In fact, at the other side of the grounds there is a tree that must have been struck by lightning, I think. The Hollow Tree is sending sugars through its roots, keeping it alive."

"All trees do that," says Gran.

"That's incredible."

"That's nature, sweetheart."

"I want to restore the trees I scorched running through the woodland. I didn't mean to. I can't bear to think of them singed and in pain."

"Push your fingers into the ground, focus on the pathway you took and feed the trees."

So I do, pushing my fingers into the soil. I picture the pathway I took with Griffin, Alpha and the pack. I imagine them renewing, growing, but am unsure it is actually working.

"I've a lot to learn, haven't I?" I say pulling my fingers out. I turn to look at Gran, then re-position my head on her shoulders.

"That you do," she says kissing my forehead. "We never stop learning, Hannah. Even at my age."

"By the way, happy birthday, Gran."

"I didn't think you'd remember, Hannah. Thank you."

"How can I forget? It's officially Halloween, after all," I smirk.

"Another year older. But I can't say that – in light of

recent events – I am more the wiser."

"Joyce told me she offered to buy you a mobile. You could have just texted, you know that, don't you?"

"I do now."

"And there's me thinking that you know absolutely everything already, Gran."

"Well, that sounds a tad over the top. Nobody knows everything. Not even Gaia," she winks. "Now, dearest. There is something I must show you, so up you get. We need to get inside the tree."

I feel a sudden excitement strike me. *We can go inside it?*

"Right, walk around the base of the trunk, feeling your way as you go. When you feel a pulling sensation, push into it. That is your entrance. I will find my own."

*Her own? Strange. Surely we would use the same.*

I follow Gran's instructions exactly as she said. I run my fingers, slowly at first, up and down the trunk searching for the feeling. Where is it? I turn to find Gran, but she has vanished. *Inside already?* I rest my hand back on the bark and the pull stings my fingers. I push against it.

*Thud!*

*Ow!*

"Perhaps a little more grace next time, Hannah," says Gran pulling me up from the floor, a huge grin stuck to her face. "You'll get used to it though."

WHITE GOLD

I, on the other hand, am not as amused as she is.

"Sorry, sweetheart. I really shouldn't laugh. There's just something genuinely funny about people falling over. Not when they've really hurt themselves, of course. But still, falling is funny."

I see her point. I snigger because I'd probably laugh, too.

I look around inside the Hollow Tree and it looks exactly like I expected. More bark and leaves, but then something catches my eye. A pile of silver fur curled into a ball. *Alpha!*

"She found her way in before you did."

Then I remember. "Didn't you have something you wanted to show me?"

"Two things, actually. Here, sit on that memory stump."

"Memory what?"

"Memory stump. It's the stump of a tree that remembers its home and returns there. All very simple."

*Really? She's got to be kidding.*

I sit down and suddenly realise I haven't got my phone with me.

"Oh my God, where's my phone. I need it."

"Gadget obsessed you youngsters are."

"No, you don't understand. It's got photos of me and Mum on it. Our holiday. Stratford. Christmas. I can't lose it."

*I've lost too much already.*

257

"Okay, pat your gown down and concentrate on a warm cosy feeling as you do it."

I look at Gran, baffled. Her eyes answer. *Trust me*, they say.

I imagine being laid on the grass in our garden at home baking in the sunshine, then begin patting the gown. I keep my eyes closed, but have a sudden feeling like a weight is lifting. I keep patting the entire dress then open my eyes. I'm surrounded by a huge pile of leaves, left in my jumper and jeans. I pat my back pocket. Yes! I pull my phone from my jeans, and stare at my screensaver, pressing the home button every time Mum's image fades. I realise I have kept a voicemail Mum left me just a few days ago. But I mustn't replay it. Not yet. I flick through the last batch of selfies we had taken whilst shopping for her birthday. I look at the battery bar. Not red yet. I have no idea where my charger is, so turn it off.

*I will only turn it on when I'm absolutely desperate.*

That phone is my lifeline to her. It's not like I'm anywhere near home. York is nearly 200 miles away. No photographs on walls I can cling to, here. No clothes of hers I can bury myself in. No perfume to spray remembering her scent. Our house will be growing cold now and I have no idea when Mum or I will ever see it again. My eyes glaze as I fight back the tears.

Alpha stirs. Maybe she is detecting my feelings. Dogs can do that, so maybe foxes can, too. I tell her to sleep a little longer.

Gran joins me on the memory stump and weaves her fingers with mine. Mum wouldn't want me to cry, apparently. Joyce must have said it a dozen times last night before we left. But how does she know? How does anyone know what our loved ones want when they aren't here to tell us themselves? No one knows. And if I want to cry, then I soddin' well will.

*'Betta art than in, lass.'*

Something Dad used to say, thickening his Yorkshire accent. It's about the only thing I agree with him on.

"Now, close your eyes. Hold out your right hand."

Gran turns my hand over, palm down. No more safety pins tearing my flesh apart I hope. I feel her slip something onto my finger and I know immediately what it is.

"Thanks, Gran," I say opening to see a flash of silver.

"Your mother wore that ring for about thirty years. In fact, she was about your age when she got it."

*It wasn't her wedding ring.* That she got rid of a long time ago.

"I love it. I love silver."

"It's not silver, sweetheart. White gold. She would want you to look after it whilst she sleeps."

"Is she sleeping?"

"Yes. Yes, she is. We will see her again, Hannah. I believe that and so must you. I know you miss her. I miss her incredibly. But we mustn't mourn her. She isn't dead. She's just someplace else right now."

"Can I ask a question? Although, you probably already know it."

"To be honest, it has been harder reading your thoughts since we arrived here and I have purposefully tried to keep out. So, no. What is your question?"

"What about Evelyn? Is she alive? Did she make it back to her family?"

"I believe we will find the answers here because of what I am about to show you, Hannah."

"And Galtonia? Will she come back?"

"Now that, I don't know."

"But she knows everything, Gran."

"No, not everything."

"But what if she's found a way back through the jigsaw? What if she finds Mum?"

"She won't. No one knows about Caroline being interred under Windsor House, only us and Joyce. Like I said, I believe all the answers lie here. But even those answers must wait their turn because we have an appointment with a little girl."

"A little girl?" I ask confused, as Gran waves her arms across a small pile of logs in the middle of the floor, igniting a fire.

"Yes. Her name is Harriet."

Harriet?

Gran dips her fingertips into the flames. What!

Then, just as Evelyn did, Gran begins skywriting, flicking her wrist to and fro creating shapes. In no time at all, Gran, the seamstress, has cut into the fabric of the world's quilt. Above the fire, another jigsaw has appeared, although Gran calls it a Hollow. *A hollow inside the Hollow Tree.*

I shuffle forward, straining to see through it. Eventually, my eyes adjust to a small fragment of moonlight, which looks like it's peeking in through a crack in some curtains. I cannot see the rest of the room, but in the middle of the window of light, I see her.

"Who is she, Gran?"

"*My* Grandmother."

# Enjoyed this book?

Reviews are the most powerful tools in my arsenal as an independent author. I don't have the might or muscle that the traditional publishing houses do. I can't take out full-page ads in newspapers or even grace the first tables that greet you as you walk into some of the big bookstores - not yet anyway!

But I want to build something more powerful - and as incredible as Hannah herself - that is a bunch of fabulous, loyal and committed readers. Building this takes a lot of hard work. Honest reviews of my books help bring the attention of other readers like yourself.

So, if you enjoyed this first book in The Earth Chronicles series, I would be grateful if you could spend just a couple of minutes leaving a review.

You can also sign up to my mailing list at www.jabrowne. com and be one of the first to hear about competitions, events and all the latest news from me. Most importantly, the release date for *The Earth Chronicles: Gaia's Revenge*.

Turn the page for an extract.

# Coming – Spring 2019

*The Earth Chronicles:*
*Gaia's Revenge*

*"Nature favours those organisms which leave the environment in better shape for their progeny to survive."*
James Lovelock

# Earth – Halloween: Hannah

## Chapter One

### Inferno

I am not at home in bed. I can't roll over and pull the duvet over my head or flick my electric blanket on. I'm a Northerner. Tough things out mostly, but sometimes, just sometimes, it's really nice to flick the leccy blanket on. But I'm not cold here, lying on the ground. Blades of grass tickle my palms as I entwine my fingers amongst them. Strange. October doesn't feel so cold today. I inhale the aroma of pines and the lemony scent of fir trees which triggers my hunger clock. As I roll over onto my stomach I imagine what delicious treats Gran can rustle up for us. I push myself up onto my knees, which brings me face to face with it. Etched words that can't be unread and I wish, more than anything else in the world, that I'd suddenly lost my ability to read.

Engraved into stone.

Burned into my brain.

These words have robbed me of my ability to breathe.

*But she isn't dead …*

HERE LIES CAROLINE WALSINGHAM

BELOVED DAUGHTER AND MOTHER.

TIME PASSES, BUT LOVE STAYS.

BORN: 30TH SEPTEMBER 1976

DIED: ALL HALLOWS' EVE

I don't understand. I don't understand because she's not dead. My mother isn't dead. *She just isn't.* Gran wouldn't lie to me. *Would she?*

I crawl forwards. My hands register the sudden coldness of the grass. Dew soaks through my jeans. *How is that possible? It was warm.* I reach out, fingers connect and trace the grooves like reading Braille because my eyes just won't accept what they see.

"Here lies Caroline Walsingham." My voice barely audible.

That isn't possible.

"Time passes but love stays."

Of course love stays. It doesn't just go! Defiance awakens deep from inside me.

"But time hasn't passed!" I shout. "She's just sleeping."

We interred Mum's body under Windsor House. Me and Joyce and Gran. *Where is Gran?*

I call out to her through gritted teeth. Gripping the headstone to steady myself, I glance around but see only trees, clustered together in a silence that slaps me.

*But I felt Mum's heartbeat. That's how I'd known she was alive!* Did Gran lie to me? Is Mum de – My whole body trembles. *I need to run.* Like running will save my life. Or Mum's.

*Where the soddin' hell is Gran?*

I want to swear, but Gran hates swearing.

"GRAN?"

I stand and the world swirls around me and it's then that it registers; I'm in the gardens at the front of Windsor House. *But we were inside the Hollow Tree watching Harriet. How did I get here?* I glance in the direction of where I think the Hollow Tree is but suddenly every tree looks the same, like sentries on guard in rank and file, Gran used to say. There're so many. *Shouldn't I just know which it is?* It's *my* Hollow Tree after all. Or, did I dream it all? Am I dreaming now?

Light travels faster than sound so I see the flash millionths of a second before the wall of noise strikes my chest, launching me into the air.

*Urgh! What the hell?*

Hitting the ground so hard steals every inch of breath from my body. If I knew what being drunk felt like, I would imagine it could be like this. Sick. Dizzy. Sick. I roll onto my side and try to focus but a rush of warmth flows down my head. I clasp my hand to the back of my skull. It's wet and warm. I look down at the blood seeping through my fingers. Tears begin streaming, washing away the grit that has invaded my eyes. I try to focus on something. Anything. Something that looks like anything. I scramble backward away from the intense heat stinging my cheeks. As the ringing in my ears begins to fade, I clutch my mouth, biting down. Don't throw up. My vision clears enough to register what happened. I stand, feeling the size of David facing a

Goliath-sized wall of fire.

No! No! NO!

"MUM!"

Pushing myself up, I dart towards the house but searing heat forces me back. *Argh!* Every second the human brain has one hundred thousand chemical reactions. Every single one of mine adds up to just one thing – Mum!

"Gran, where are you? Help me! Help me!"

I spin around and scream out towards the mass of moonlit trees begging for Gran.

"Help me!" I choke.

Smoke billows up to mingle with the darkest clouds. Eyes closed, I push my thoughts out to Gran with every ounce of energy I can muster.

"The house is on fire. Please, Gran! Mum's inside! Joyce! Oh my God, Joyce! The foxes! They'll die! Do something!"

Nothing.

*This can't be happening.* What do I do?

Almost as soon as the tears fall, the searing heat dries their track marks. *Get a grip! I have to do something.*

I charge at the house again through a smoke-filled haze which engulfs it, but thick flames just lick and lap the air which feeds its greed as it grows and grows.

"No! Mum! Joyce!"

*How do I stop this?*

Blisters form across my knuckles, as I smash my fists

into the ground. Screams rip from my chest over and over. My eyes glaze against the glow of the fire destroying Windsor House. Destroying the place where Mum's body lies cocooned. But her conscious, her soul isn't there. Will she feel the fire? Will she know?

*She couldn't have survived that. She must be dead.*

I collapse and feel the coldness of the earth's bed seep through my skin. A blanket of smoke settles on my chest.

I'm dying.

Wait for me, Mum.

# About the Author

J. A. Browne is the author of *The Earth Chronicles* series. *Hannah and the Hollow Tree* is her debut children's novel and first in series. She is also a primary school teacher in Yorkshire with a passion for the environment, animals and all things nature. J. A. Browne lives in Calderdale with her husband and can often be found running around the countryside dreaming up new plot ideas for her characters.

There are lots of ways you can contact her:
Her online home is www.jabrowne.com
She would love to connect with you by email:
author@jabrowne.com, or on Instagram @jabrowneauthor
Alternatively, you can tweet her a message @JABrowne2017 or find her on Facebook at https://www.facebook.com/JABrowne

# Acknowledgements

It has taken over a decade to bring this book to life and there have been many wonderful people along the way who have encouraged, supported and guided me in the process. Firstly, I am indebted to the inspiring, passionate and talented Darran Holmes for his magical illustrations. It has been a privilege.

A huge thank you to my editor Carly Corlett at Peahen Publishing whose wisdom and guidance have been invaluable and Nicola Moore for her skills in designing the book cover, which I adore.

Many thanks to Leeds Trinity University Creative Writing MA tutors, Martyn Bedford, Paul "Oz" Hardwick, Amina Alyal and students for their tremendous guidance and passion for the written word. A special thank you goes to Joyce Simpson, former Head of English at LTU whose expertise and love for children's literature reignited mine. To Mark Dawson and James Blatch for always championing independent authors and to James Lovelock for awakening us all to Gaia.

To so many wonderful friends who always leave an imprint on me for their strength, compassion, determination and love. Sonia, Sharon, Angela, Tracy, Denise and Joan.

Thank you to my family, Stephen, Janette, Carol, Trevor, Rob, Hannah, Courtney, Joshua, Oliver, Scarlet, Veronica, Wingrove, Bethany, Benjamin, Reuben, Jacqueline, Dean and Amie.

A heartfelt thank you goes to Maria Stephenson and my husband, Aaron Browne, my soul mates in literature and life. Without you, this journey would never have continued. And finally, my Mum and Dad, Grandma Eva and Grandma Mabel – where it all began. Love stays.